From the Files of

Read all the books about *Madison Finn*!

Coming Soon!

Don't miss Super Edition #1

From the Files of

Madison Finn

All That Glitters

By Laura Dower

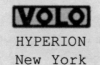

HYPERION
New York

For Myles and Olivia,
my stars

Text copyright © 2005 by Laura Dower

From the Files of Madison Finn and the Volo colophon are trademarks of Disney Enterprises, Inc.
Volo® is a registered trademark of Disney Enterprises, Inc.

Printed in the United States of America

First Edition
1 3 5 7 9 10 8 6 4 2

The main body of text of this book is set in 13-point Frutiger Roman.

ISBN 0-7868-5688-2

Visit www.hyperionbooksforchildren.com

Chapter 1

"Your office looks like a train wreck," Madison mumbled as she handed Mom a stack of empty file folders. "How do you expect me to keep my room clean when you leave stuff all over *your* room?"

"Honey bear, you know I've been busy," Mom grumbled. "I've got a big business trip coming up, and there's paperwork and hours of video to log . . ."

"Busy? Mom, you never let *me* get away with that excuse," Madison said.

Madison's pug, Phineas T. Finn, let out a loud yawn and started to snort as if he were about to sneeze but couldn't quite do it.

"Look!" Mom chuckled. "Even Phin thinks you're being unreasonable."

Madison couldn't help laughing. Phin's little snorts came fast and furious until he finally let out one big doggy sneeze. Spray flew everywhere.

"Phinnie!" Madison cried. "Gross! I wish I could teach you how to blow your nose into a tissue."

Mom handed Madison a pile of books from her shelf. "Do you want these?" she asked. Madison realized she was holding a stack of old Nancy Drew books. Mom had collected them as a child. Some of the bindings were cracked. The pages had yellowed and torn in places. But Madison didn't mind folded-over corners on pages or even handwriting inside a book. She believed that books weren't really good unless they'd been read a hundred times at least.

"Maybe I'll reorganize my bookshelves this afternoon," Madison mused.

"Why don't you take Phin for a walk instead?" Mom suggested. The dog wagged his tail, readying himself for sneeze number two. "Get out of the house for a while. Go over to Aimee's house and play with Blossom."

Aimee Gillespie was one of Madison's best friends at Far Hills Junior High—and a fellow dog owner. Aimee's basset hound, Blossom, and Madison's Phin were like dog best friends, if there were such a thing.

"I can't meet Aimee. She's at dance class today," Madison said.

But Madison agreed that getting outside was a good idea—with or without her friend. She grabbed one of Phin's rawhide chews and a rope toy. Phin's collar clinked as Madison attached the leash and tugged him toward the front door.

"We can go over to Far Hills Park," Madison announced as she pulled on her jacket. "We haven't checked out the dog run yet."

"Great idea!" Mom said.

Madison loved the fact that the town had finally erected a special fence around a section of the park and marked it RESERVED FOR DOGS. It was covered with patches of grass and dirt where dogs could run and sniff and play long games of fetch. It was also a place where dog owners could go and hang out together.

En route to the park, Phin trotted along, pug nose in the air, stopping only to sniff at the occasional hydrant or mailbox. He knew what was coming; Phin loved nothing better than the company of other dogs.

"Howwooooooooo!"

As they turned in to the park, heading toward the dog run, a loose hound dog let out a wild howl. Madison recognized the pooch from the neighborhood. His name was Red, and his owner was also a volunteer at the Far Hills Animal Shelter, where Madison sometimes worked after school. When he saw Madison, Red's owner gave a huge wave.

Phin pulled hard on his leash, and as they reached the gate to the dog run, Madison unclipped it so he could run free. He dodged a barking

Labrador retriever and sniffed his way over toward a white fluffy dog, probably a Maltese.

"Fluffy!" the dog's owner called out, looking terrified.

"It's okay, you don't have to worry. Phinnie's a good dog," Madison reassured the woman.

Phin and Fluffy stepped around each other, noses sniffing madly, whiskers twitching, ears wiggling. It was like some kind of mating dance.

"Finnster! Finnster! Over here!"

Madison jerked her head around. Finnster was one of her many nicknames. Actually, it was a special name given to her by Hart Jones, one of her seventh-grade classmates. And right now, Hart was there. He was walking along one of the pathways through the park with another one of Madison's guy friends, Drew Maxwell.

Madison's heart skipped a beat. She and Hart had been "in like" this year, doing their own version of a mating dance. First they'd pretend to be cool about their relationship, and then they'd act like good friends, and then finally they would admit that yes, they really, really did want to go on a real date together. Of course, nothing had happened yet in the date department. Her friends were growing impatient with their behavior. Everyone knew about the mutual crush and wondered why Madison and Hart didn't just act more like a couple.

But for whatever reason, they didn't. Madison

figured they were both a little scared. After all, it *was* scary to like someone that much. It was scary to hear Hart calling her name in the middle of the park, too.

"Finnster! What's up?" Hart's voice boomed again.

Madison shrugged and gave the two boys a wide smile. They came closer toward her, arms swinging. They each carried a pair of black skates. Hart had two hockey sticks with him, too.

Madison pushed a strand of hair behind her ear. Were her lips chapped? Was she wearing something cute? She glanced down at her purple sweatpants and sneakers.

"Are you here with Phin?" Drew asked, leaning over the dog-run fence. No one could enter the area without a dog, so the boys stayed on the other side.

"Yeah, I'm here with Phinnie," Madison said meekly. She pointed in the direction of Phin, who was still playing with Fluffy. "We went for a long walk. I was helping my mom clean out the office, and . . . well, you probably don't care what I was doing."

"Sure we care," Hart said. He leaned the hockey sticks against the fence. "We saw you from the path."

"We were over at the rink," Drew said.

"Yeah, I figured," Madison said, nodding at the skates and sticks.

"Duh," Hart said. "Of course."

"I was going to call you today, Maddie," Drew said.

"Call me?" Madison repeated.

"I invited everyone over to my house this afternoon; sort of a last-minute thing. We thought of it when we were playing hockey. Want to come?"

"Yeah," Hart said. He shoved his hands in his pockets. "I'll be there," he added cheerily.

Madison didn't know how to answer. It was one of those scary moments. If she had been honest with herself—and with everyone else, especially Hart—she would have jumped right over the dog-run fence, fallen into Hart's arms, and declared, *"You'll be there? Well, let's go right now!"*

Instead, she rocked from one foot to the other and briefly glanced back over at Phin, who had moved from Fluffy to a sheepdog five times his size. Phin's curlicue tail was wagging, so Madison left him alone. With his tail still moving, Phin ran over to a pair of dachshunds.

"Well?" Drew asked expectantly. Madison had still not responded to his invitation.

"Well . . . okay," Madison replied. "I just have to take Phin home and my Mom can drive me over."

Hart's face lit up. "Cool!" he said, clapping his hands.

"Come over around four," Drew said. "My mom will probably order pizzas or something if you want to stay for supper. And we can watch a movie, too."

Drew Maxwell's family had their very own screening room. They were one of the wealthiest families in Far Hills; their house also had a giant pool, tennis court, and about a dozen bedrooms. Drew's parents basically let him do whatever he wanted, and he loved having his friends over for parties or study sessions.

"I'll call you if my mom says no for some reason," Madison said.

"She won't say no," Hart said.

"Okay," Madison giggled. "So I'll see you later, then."

The boys grabbed their stuff and headed back toward the path. Just then, Phinnie darted between Madison's legs. He was being chased by three other dogs. Madison felt her feet go out from under her. She briefly flew up into the air, knocked into the side of the fence, and landed on her butt—right on the cold, hard dirt.

"Oh, my!" From across the dog run, Fluffy's owner ran over to Madison, arms flailing. "Are you all right?"

Red's owner ran over, too, to offer his helping hand.

Madison rubbed her backside and stood up. She felt a little wobbly, but nothing seemed broken or bruised. She glanced at the spot where Drew and

Hart had been. Happily, her crush had not witnessed her pratfall. She kindly thanked the other dog owners and reattached Phin's leash. It was time to go.

The walk home from the dog run seemed to take forever. When Madison and Phin finally reached the front porch of their home on Blueberry Street, Phin was panting from all of his afternoon activity. Madison was panting a little, too, in expectation. A get-together at Drew's was about to turn her boring Saturday into something extraordinary.

Mom said it was fine to go over to Drew's house for movies and dinner. She would drop Madison off and pick her up afterward.

"Who else is going?" Mom asked. "What about Fiona and Chet?"

Fiona Waters and her twin brother, Chet, were other friends of Madison's from school and the neighborhood. They lived only a few streets away. Mom wanted to offer everyone a ride.

Madison shrugged at Mom's questions. "Drew said everyone was going. I mean, I guess Aimee won't be there, because of Dance. But let me call Fiona and see what's up."

Fiona's phone rang and rang. Her answering machine wasn't working, and no one picked up.

I wonder where she is, Madison thought. She guessed that maybe Chet, Fiona, and Egg, Madison's best guy friend and Fiona's "boyfriend," were already on their way to Drew's house. That meant she needed to hurry up.

Madison raced up to her bedroom to change out of the sweatpants into a more festive outfit. She pulled on three different T-shirts before deciding upon a pink one with little rhinestones on it in the shape of a heart. She tucked the shirt into a pair of jeans with a thick belt and topped it off with a snug pink sweater. It looked like a short cardigan from the pages of some fashion magazine, but it was actually a sweater that Madison's Gramma Helen had knitted for her that fall. Each button was in the shape of a flower, carved out of mother-of-pearl. Madison finished the outfit with a pair of dark pink stretch cable socks and some clogs. Then she applied her favorite strawberry-kiwi lip gloss.

"Don't you look gorgeous!" Mom said as Madison pulled her jacket on over the sweater and shirt.

Madison grinned. "I'd better," she said.

"Oh, I see," Mom said. She understood. "Hart's going to be there, isn't he?"

Madison blushed. "Yes."

"At least all your friends will be there, too, so you won't have to get too nervous or embarrassed," Mom said, stroking Madison's now-pink cheek. "I know that one of these days he'll pop the question."

"Mom!" Madison cried.

"You know what I mean," Mom said.

Phin let out another snort and sneeze as they walked through the back door and headed for the car. Mom had been right about Madison's nerves. When Madison bent down to lift Phin into the back-seat for the drive over to Drew's house, she nearly dropped him. It was a talking-about-Hart aftershock. Lately, that topic of conversation had been making Madison extra twitchy.

After the drive across town to Drew's megaman-sion, however, Madison tried to get her twitches in check. She rang the doorbell and took a deep, deep breath, just in case Hart answered the door.

"You're here!" Drew cried in a very loud voice. Music blared in the background.

"Wow, some party," Madison said. "Is everyone here?"

"You bet," Drew said. "Mom's making cheddar-cheese popcorn and milk shakes for us."

"Sounds good," Madison said. She knew Fiona would be into that menu. Fiona ate anything. Aimee, on the other hand, ate like a rabbit. She wouldn't pig out on anything but tofu, salad, or granola. The Gillespies were health nuts.

Madison followed Drew inside and down a set of stairs to the screening room.

"Everyone's waiting," he said as he opened the door. The music sounded even louder from there.

Madison adjusted the waistband of her jeans. Even though she liked the low-rider style, sometimes the pants slipped a little too far down. She wriggled around in an attempt to get comfortable. It would be *so* nice to grab Fiona's hand and let go of all of her nervousness.

"Howdy, you!" a voice chirped as soon as the door flew open. It was Elaine, a friend (actually, a girlfriend) of Drew's from down the street. She didn't attend FHJH, but sometimes she came to Drew's parties or met Madison and her friends at the town pool or at Freeze Palace, one of their favorite hangouts.

Madison said hello to Elaine and then glanced around the room, looking for other guests.

But there were none.

"Drew . . . wait . . ." Madison stammered. "I thought . . . I thought you said this was a party . . ."

"It is a party!" a new voice said.

Madison turned to see Hart standing there. Her stomach flip-flopped. Was this some kind of setup? What *was* this?

"Good thing we ran into you in the park," Hart said.

"Good thing," Madison replied, still unsure about what was going on. Where was the "every-one" that Drew had mentioned? Had they all conveniently canceled at the last minute? Had anyone else ever even been invited?

"You have to come inside and see something," Hart said. He reached out and touched Madison's shoulder when he spoke. She thought her legs would turn to jelly.

"Look!" Hart cried. "Just look at all of Drew's new DVDs. It's amazing!"

"He's building a collection," Elaine said. She was now standing next to them. "Drew's mother just bought him *Matrix*, *Star Wars*, and *The Lord of the Rings* boxed sets."

"Really?" Madison said, still unsteady and now very unsure about what was going on. She wanted to run. Or call Mom. Or scream?

Ding-a-ling-a-ling.

"What was that?" Hart asked Drew.

"New doorbell," Drew replied.

"When did you get a new doorbell?" Madison asked.

"Mom wanted one that played Mozart, but she settled for a cooler 'ding' noise. You know how she is," Drew explained.

"Drew! Darling!" Drew's mother's voice called out from upstairs. "You have more company!"

Madison felt a great sense of relief. Everyone really was there now. She wasn't trapped in the middle of some secret double date.

Whew.

She heard Egg's voice; he was making an obnoxious crack. Walter "Egg" Diaz often went out of his way to be obnoxious. Madison hoped that Egg's arrival meant that Fiona had arrived, too. Sure enough, a few moments later, Fiona bounded down the stairs and into the screening room.

The two BFFs embraced.

Moments later, Dan Ginsburg, another friend from both school and the animal clinic, arrived. He'd brought a few CDs to listen to, and Drew popped them into the stereo immediately.

Everyone started goofing around, moving their hips and clapping to the music. Hart stood across from Madison, a wide smile on his face.

Madison felt as if they were at a fifth-grade school dance. She leaned back against the wall. Where was Fiona? She could feel the drumbeat of Drew's speakers.

Boom, boom, boom.

Inside her chest, Madison's heart was making the exact same noise.

Chapter 2

From: MadFinn
To: Bigwheels
Subject: Trouble with Hart?
Date: Sat 5 Dec 9:12 PM

OK. I just spent Sat. afternoon w/Hart--the supposed crush of my life (yeah, well, in my dreams)--and here's the deal: he was paying attention to me the ENTIRE time-- and everyone witnessed it--and he even held my hand at one point-- and I still have NO idea what's

really going on between us. Did
today really happen?

I should get it--well, him--by
now. I mean I went over to my
friend Drew's place expecting a
zillion people and then the only
person there other than Drew and
his gf Elaine was Hart. Duh. And
then Drew was falling all over
Elaine with this incredibly doofy
laugh and grabbing for her hands,
while Hart and I just stood there
LA LA LA. And when all the other
people finally arrived, the only
place to sit was practically on
Hart's lap. They fixed it that
way, I could tell. And then we all
ate pizza and Hart asked me if he
could try a bite of mine, which
was kind of gross but kind of
romantic in a sharing way. And
then Drew's mom put in one of his
new DVDs and turned the lights
down in their screening room (my
mom would never have approved of
that) but there I was again
sitting with the one and only
Hart practically knee to knee--I
swear--my knee touching his knee.
Touching!

But in spite of all this, he didn't ask me out. He didn't say anything specific about dating or whatever. Grrrrr. Why, after all this time, are Hart and I still not a WE?

Am I cursed around guys or what?

You know my lame-o history. I had that first real kiss (OMG it was soooo fun) with that kid Mark from my gramma's place in Chicago. But a first kiss is supposed to be one of those over-the-moon, can't-sleep, last-forever kind of things, but mine only lasted like a week for me. A week? Huh? Then I double-crushed on that Josh guy who lives next door (until I found out he was already dating another ninth grader--hello!) And then I went skiing with Aim and decided to blow off liking Hart AGAIN. But no matter what I think or do or say, I still come back to this place, this crush. Why is it so hard to stop liking someone once you start? Liking Hart is like diving into a mudslide or maybe quicksand. Glug, glug, GLUG.

Maybe all of this waiting means
something. Like Hart is THE ONE,
as in, the guy I'm destined to be
with. Got any advice 4 me?

Oh, and BTW how r u?

Yours till the boy friends,*

Maddie

*note that this is not yours till
the break ups or yours till the kiss
offs or yours till the c u laters--I
still DO I DO I DO have hope LOL

Madison hit SEND and waited for her screen to
flash. After a split second it beeped, which meant
that the message had gone through. Then Madison
hit a few more keys on her laptop and exited her
e-mailbox. She wanted to visit her favorite Web site,
bigfishbowl.com. The headline on this Web page
flashed in neon letters: ASK THE BLOWFISH.

Madison clicked on a teeny, yellow-striped fish
swimming on-screen. A cursor popped up, and
Madison stared at the row of blank spaces where she
was meant to write an important question. Slowly,
she typed her question into the space and waited for
the Blowfish to reply.

What is going on with me and Hart?

Madison sighed. She tapped her fingers on the desk and impatiently watched the tiny clock on the computer screen. Time was passing slower than slowly. Where was her answer? A restless Phin, who had been curled up by her feet, scrambled across the carpet and hopped onto Madison's window seat. He stared across the room at her as she waited until the answer finally appeared.

You are swimming in a flood.

"No way! A flood?" Madison cried. "What is that supposed to mean, Phinnie? This Web site is so messed up sometimes. . . ."

She leaned back away from her laptop and let out a big sigh. Phin jumped from the window seat and then scurried over to the doorjamb and then made a beeline for the top of Madison's bed. He was restless.

Madison reworded her question and retyped it into the blank space.

Will Hart and I ever go on a real date?

The Blowfish hummed, or at least Madison's computer did. It hummed and sizzled and chugged. She waited another minute for another answer. At last it popped up.

The tide has turned.

"Huh?"

That answer wasn't good enough for Madison, either, so she tried one last question. Now she was as direct as possible.

Tell me if Hart wants to be my boyfriend—RIGHT NOW.

The Blowfish took its time again. But its answer finally appeared on the screen in glowing yellow letters.

Most decidedly yes when the water is rising.

Madison buried her head in her hands. Yes? Rising water? She was good at English but she was no code breaker. Then again, how could she actually believe that a computer could tell her whether or not the crush of her life would come through in the clutch?

Obviously it couldn't. Duh.

Just then, Phin woofed and flopped onto his back atop Madison's bed. He rubbed and rolled and then took one of the throw pillows that had been on top of Madison's comforter in his teeth and shook it.

"Rarrrrrrrrrgrrrrr!"

"Phinnie! No-o-o-o-o!" Madison cried.

It was too late. The bed was completely unmade. Everything that had been on top now lay in a messy pile on the floor: a notebook, her latest copy of *Star Beat* magazine, her math textbook, and a small pile of new mail. Madison bent over to pick the things up.

That was when she saw something shimmer. On the front of a bright, glittery, oversized pink envelope, written in dark purple cursive letters was

Madison's name and address. In the upper left corner was a doodle of a heart with the letters *NYC* inside it.

Madison grabbed the pink envelope and tore it open.

**You're Invited
to a Last-Minute Party
Lindsay Frost's 13th Birthday Weekend
What? Two overnights in the city
with Lindsay and a few friends
(We will be shopping, sight-seeing,
and other stuff!)
When? Friday & Saturday, December 11 & 12
Where? New York City
Lindsay's aunt Mimi Frost's pad
The Manhattan Towers, East 82nd Street, PH B
RSVP to Lindsay ASAP**

A party! Madison's pulse revved up. She couldn't believe how perfect this invitation was. It was the perfect thing to take her mind off (*way* off) Hart Jones.

Clutching the invitation in one hand, Madison raced out of her bedroom and downstairs to find Mom, who was curled up in a ball in front of the television set. Phin trotted right behind, panting and wondering about all the fuss.

"Mo-o-o-o-om!" Madison called out, breathless. "Did you see this in my mail?"

Mom glanced up at the pink-glitter invitation and smiled. "Yes, I wondered about that. I didn't see a return address. Who sent it?"

"Lindsay is having a party. A birthday party in New York City. Can you believe it?"

"Wow, that's nice. Is it a lunch or something during the day?" Mom asked.

Madison shook her head. "Actually, it's a sleepover."

"Oh?" Mom frowned a little bit.

"Mom, you have to let me go. First of all, Lindsay is one of my best, best friends. Second of all, it sounds like so much fun."

"Hmmm. I don't know. A sleepover in the city? Where are you girls planning to stay? Let me see the invitation."

Madison handed the card over and waited for Mom to read it.

"Maybe I should call Mrs. Frost and ask her about this," Mom said.

"Oh, Mom, the party is at Lindsay's aunt's apartment, so there'll be a chaperone at all times," Madison cried. "And Lindsay's aunt is this very cool lady who has all these cool clothes, and she knows all the cool places to go and . . ."

21

"Gee. Sounds cool," Mom said drily.

"Very funny, Mom," Madison said, getting the joke.

"Well . . ."

Mom took her time responding. She eyed the invitation again.

"Okay, honey bear," Mom finally said. "You've convinced me. You can go. I'll call Lindsay's mom later just to double-check everything."

Madison lunged forward and threw her arms around Mom's neck.

"Thank you. Thank you. Thank you!" Madison gushed. "You are the best. I won't get into trouble, I swear, and we won't do too much shopping and . . ."

"Maddie, slow down," Mom chuckled. "I know you'll be good. I trust you. But you had better start packing. I know how long that takes."

Madison felt giddy. Mom was letting her go! She wondered who else would be attending the party. Had Lindsay invited everyone in their class? No, that wasn't possible. Maybe just the BFFs—Madison, Aimee, and Fiona? That seemed more likely. Madison needed to speak to Lindsay right away and get all of the particulars.

As Mom went into the kitchen to get a snack for Phin, Madison grabbed the portable phone sitting atop a table in the living room.

"Hello-o-o-o!" an unfamiliar voice trilled. "Frost residence."

"Um . . . hello," Madison said, pausing. "Who's this?"

"Who is *this*?" the voice replied. "Is this a friend of Lindsay's?"

"Um . . . yes," Madison said meekly.

"Well, howdy-doodle! I'm Lindsay's aunt Mimi," she said. "Sorry to say that lovely Lindsay's not in right now. But I can take a message."

Madison couldn't help smiling at every word Mimi said. Each sentence came out like a little song.

"Are you the Aunt Mimi who lives in the city?" Madison asked.

"*C'est moi!* The one and only," Mimi said.

"I've heard a lot about you. Lindsay always tells us funny stories. . . ."

"Lo-o-o-ove it!" Mimi shrieked. Madison had to hold the phone away from her ear.

Lindsay had spoken a lot about her crazy aunt in Manhattan, who had a vault full of money that she had earned playing the stock market, among other things. According to Lindsay, Aunt Mimi was like a character from a movie, complete with false eyelashes and fur hats. She had made millions developing her own "magic" brands of quick-drying mascara, shimmer powder, and other beauty items that sold like hotcakes in boutiques around the world. She called her line of products Serious Beauty, even though she wasn't serious-sounding in the least.

Apparently, Mimi had never married, although she'd dated movie stars and big shots in business all her life. She had no children of her own, but Mimi loved to spoil her niece. She spent her loot in wild ways, especially when it came to Lindsay's birthdays. One time she'd rented an entire circus tent (including a baby elephant) for Lindsay's sixth birthday. Another time Mimi had hired one of the best magicians in the city to come to Lindsay's party—and make Lindsay disappear.

"I'm glad to meet you by phone," Madison said. "Can you tell Lindsay that I called?"

"Sweetums, you haven't even told me your name!" Mimi said.

"Oh, I'm Madison Finn."

"Madison! Did you say Madison? Is this *the* Madison?"

"Um, yeah, I guess," Madison stammered, holding back the urge to giggle.

"Awww! I know you! Lindsay has told me gobs and oodles about you. My goodness! How *are* you? How's your pooch? You're the one with a pug, right?"

"Right," Madison said, impressed.

"So you'll be coming to the big glittery bash in the Big Apple!" Mimi declared. "Fah-bulous!"

"Will you tell Lindsay I called?" Madison asked.

"Hey! Does a mosquito bite?" Mimi responded. "You betcha I will!"

Madison giggled. "Thanks, Ms. Frost."

"Call me Mimi. We're practically related!"

Madison laughed again and hung up.

"Time to party!" Madison said.

She jumped in front of the hall mirror and struck a pose.

"New York City, here I come."

Chapter 3

On Monday morning at school, Madison found Fiona and Aimee near their lockers.

"Where's Lindsay?" Madison asked.

"I haven't seen her yet," Fiona said.

From around a corner, Lindsay craned her neck and yelled, "Hello, party girls!" really loudly. She was grinning from ear to ear.

"There you are!" Aimee said.

Lindsay rushed over to her friends with arms extended, and the foursome squeezed together in a group hug.

"You can all come to my party, and I am so-o-o-o psyched," Lindsay declared. "I thought for sure you would have some dance recital, Aim, or that you'd have soccer, Fiona, or that you'd have to work at the animal hospital, Maddie, or that . . ."

"Relax," Aimee said. "We're coming. All of us."

"We wouldn't miss it for the world," Fiona said.

Lindsay smiled broadly again. She held her hand up to her chest as if she were getting a little choked up, so Madison linked arms with her friend.

"Are you okay?" Madison asked.

"Yeah, I just wish it were Saturday already," Lindsay said with a laugh.

"Hold on. I just thought of something," Fiona said. "What do you want for a present, Lindsay?"

"Present? Gee, I don't know," Lindsay shrugged.

"How about hair combs?" Aimee asked. "I saw some beautiful tortoiseshell ones at the beauty shop at the mall. They would match your hair."

Lindsay shrugged. "That sounds nice."

"What about a book? You like to read," Fiona said. "Did you read *Sisterhood of the Traveling Pants* yet?"

Lindsay nodded. "I read them all."

"Wait! I know exactly what to get you," Madison said.

The idea had popped into Madison's head like a flash of lightning. She would buy one of those picture frames with a dozen different spots for various-sized photographs. During the weekend, Madison would take pictures with Dad's digital camera and then print out the good ones in the right sizes to fit the different spaces. Then she could place a collage on top of the matting inside the frame. It was the perfect place to write secret messages and cut out words from magazines. Madison knew that Fiona and Aimee would probably want to help her out, too.

"You guys," Lindsay said. "I really don't care so much about the gifts. I just want to have a good time. I've never brought friends into the city like this before. My mom keeps saying it's such a big deal. She was nervous at first, but then my aunt convinced her that everything would be okay."

"I talked to your aunt on the phone the other night," Madison said. "She sounds like a real trip."

"Yeah, to the moon," Lindsay said with another laugh. "Sometimes I feel like Aunt Mimi really is from another planet. She has the wildest ideas. I don't understand how she and my mom could be related."

"That's what I say about my brother," Fiona said. "I'm convinced that one day I'll be able to prove that we are not actually twins. I just can't be related to that moron."

Everyone laughed out loud.

The bell rang in the hallway as the girls continued to talk about the party planning. All Aimee could think about was the clothes she needed to buy. She was ready for some serious shopping. Fiona wanted to know if they would be able to visit the

Empire State Building, because she'd never been to the top before, not since she'd moved to New York from California. Madison wanted to visit the American Museum of Natural History and take a walk through Central Park.

But Lindsay didn't know *what* her Aunt Mimi had planned.

"How can you not know?" Aimee asked. "It's your birthday."

"She told me she wanted everything to be a surprise," Lindsay said.

"That sounds cool," Madison said with a grin. "What's better than a surprise?"

"I can think of a lot of things!" Aimee said. "Like knowing where we'll be shopping, for one thing."

Madison and Fiona both frowned at Aimee when she said that.

"It's Lindsay's party, Aim," Fiona said. "Not yours."

"Fine," Aimee said, letting out a little huff. "Sorry, Lindsay. I guess I'm just feeling a little carried away. My mother usually doesn't let me go into the city unless she goes, too . . . and I have this list of places I've always wanted to see . . . and . . . I guess I should just be quiet. It's *your* party."

"Maybe my aunt Mimi will take us to some of the stores you like," Lindsay said. "She knows all the best places to shop. I told her you were a dancer, and she got this look in her eye like she knew *just* the place to go."

29

"She did?" Aimee said. "Wow, that's so cool."

From down the hall, a group of ninth graders loped along toward the girls. The four friends shuffled off to the side and leaned against the locker bank.

"I hate being in the lowest grade sometimes," Fiona said.

"Me, too," Madison agreed.

Madison looked up at her friends' faces. All three stood there, mouths slightly open.

"What's wrong with you three?" Madison asked.

Lindsay just pointed. Aimee started to giggle. Fiona scowled.

"Egg!" Fiona yelled just as Madison turned around to find him holding up a sign above her head that read: KICK ME.

Madison ripped the sign out of Egg's hands. "What are you doing?" she exclaimed angrily.

Egg was nearly doubled over with laughter. Meanwhile, Madison had quickly turned three shades of plum.

"That isn't nice," Madison said, giving Egg a little punch.

Fiona grabbed Egg's arm and squeezed hard.

"I didn't even write it," Egg squealed. "Hart did! Jones wrote it. Leave me alone."

Hart came up behind Madison and threw his arm around her shoulder. "I did write it. I admit it," he said.

30

Madison froze. She could feel Hart's hand on her shoulder.

Why was he standing so close? Could he feel her bra strap through the sweater she was wearing? Could he smell her shampoo?

He kept his arm around Madison for what seemed like an eternity—and she still couldn't move. She could barely breathe.

"He thought you'd get a kick out of it," said Dan Ginsburg, who had come up behind the other boys. Standing next to him, doubled over with laughter, was Fiona's twin brother, Chet.

"That really, really wasn't nice," Fiona said again.

Madison's stomach grumbled nervously. It was like thunder, rumbling endlessly, and she hoped that no one—but especially not Hart—could hear it.

He was still standing there, twenty seconds later, with his arm around her.

"You guys are so juvenile," Aimee finally said, crossing her arms. "We were in the middle of talking, you know."

"About what, Aim?" Egg asked. "Ballet? Like you ever talk about anything else."

"Excuse me?" Aimee barked back. She looked a little stunned by Egg's comment. Everyone was. Sometimes he said things like that. Usually, the group took what he said as a joke, but that comment seemed to sting a little bit more than usual.

"You ding-dong," Aimee said to Egg. "And I

31

suppose you have so much to say about anything other than computer games. Duh."

Madison giggled, and then everyone joined in. Thankfully, Aimee had made a quick recovery.

"That was a good one," Hart said.

Madison had been so distracted by the comments flying back and forth between her friends that she hadn't noticed something very strange.

Hart *still* had his arm around her.

Soon the boys took off toward study hall, math class, and other destinations. The girls needed to do the same, but they were slower about doing it.

"What was that about?" Lindsay, Aimee, and Fiona asked, practically at the same time.

Madison shrugged. "I know. Egg was being a real jerk."

"Egg!" Aimee yelled. "Who cares about Egg? I'm talking about Hart."

"Oh," Madison said.

" 'Kick me'?" Lindsay said with a slight giggle.

Fiona smirked. "He should have put, 'Kiss me.' He was practically doing that anyway."

"*What* are you talking about?" Madison exclaimed.

"She's right, Maddie," Aimee said. "Hart was standing on top of you, like, the whole time he was here. What was going on? Did we miss something? Did you guys start dating and forget to tell us? I mean, it's been a long time coming, but really . . ."

"We are not dating," Madison asserted. "I would tell you if we were. I tell you everything."

"Everything?" Lindsay asked, raising her eyebrows.

"Lindsay!" Madison cried. She blushed instantly.

"Hart Jones wouldn't let go of your arm, Maddie," Fiona said. "I think you have to accept that. Egg even noticed. I could tell. I don't know about the other guys. Chet needs to be hit by a brick before he notices anything."

"I think you three are imagining things," Madison said.

Fiona, Aimee, and Lindsay stood there with their hands on their hips and looks of utter disbelief on their faces.

"Believe what you want to believe, Maddie," Aimee said.

"He's close," Fiona said in a high-pitched voice. "Or, as you would say, he's closer than close."

Lindsay nodded. "Yup."

"Close to *what*?" Madison asked.

No one answered in words. The three BFFs just grinned. And of course, Madison knew what Hart was close to. She'd been waiting. He'd been waiting. They'd been on the verge of this for a long time now, ever since he'd first nicknamed her Finnster, back in elementary school.

Another bell rang in the hallway. They had to dash to class but agreed to meet back at the lockers during the next free period. There was so much to talk about: the Hart incident, the party, and who knew what else.

Madison raced to her science class, which was one flight up from where they'd been standing. She readjusted the sleeve of her sweater. Hart had stretched it with all of that pulling.

"Miss Finn," Mr. Danehy said as he drummed his fingers on his desktop. "You are late. You know I don't tolerate lateness."

"I know," Madison said meekly. "Sorry."

She slinked into her assigned seat. Everyone's eyes were on her—including, from across the room, Hart's. She sensed that Hart wanted Madison to turn and smile or give him some kind of acknowledgment, but she wouldn't budge. Instead, she turned her head toward her lab partner: "Poison" Ivy Daly.

"You look awful," Ivy growled. She held one hand up, examining her manicure. "Ever consider getting a makeover?"

Madison's stomach was still grumbling. This time, it was heard—by the enemy, of all people.

"What did you have for lunch?" Ivy joked. "Should I be worried?"

Madison pressed her hands over her face. She felt hot and clammy at the same time. Was it possible for so many embarrassing, torturous events to happen simultaneously?

Apparently, yes.

No sooner had Ivy made her crack about Madison's makeover and her growling tummy than Mr. Danehy clicked his ruler on his desk.

"Attention, students," he said. He called on one of the kids in the front row to help him distribute some printouts to everyone in the class.

As the printouts were distributed, Mr. Danehy continued to speak.

"What you have in front of you is an important document," he said. "The school district has decided to give some practice standardized tests next week, starting on Monday. This sheet has the order of the testing. There is no specific study manual, but I assume you will all do your best to prepare."

"Huh?" Madison said aloud without even realizing it. "How can we prepare for something when we don't know what it is?"

A couple of other kids in the class seemed to concur.

Mr. Danehy scratched his head. "I suppose you're right, Miss Finn, but I'm afraid I don't control the test."

A silence hung over the room. Kids fidgeted in their chairs and absentmindedly flipped through their *Earth Science Is for Everyone* textbooks.

Madison quickly glanced in Hart's direction to see how he was dealing with the news about the test.

Hart was looking right at her.

Madison didn't know how to react. Without thinking, she stuck out her tongue.

She meant it as a sarcastic response to the news about the standardized test, of course. But Hart didn't look as though he understood. He didn't smile. He didn't say, "Oh, that's so funny, Finnster, hardy-har-har."

Hart just ran his fingers through his brown hair—and looked away.

Then Madison thought of something even worse than Hart's not understanding what she'd done.

If the big test was on Monday, what would happen to Lindsay's special birthday weekend?

Chapter 4

The Dilemma

Lindsay called me last nite b/c she was STILL wondering if maybe she should cancel her party. She was freaking out about this on Tuesday AND Wednesday and now it's Thursday and she is STILL wondering!!

I know why. Everyone knows.

Lindsay takes tests really, REALLY seriously (& of course I do too). She has this thing about having a perfect grade point average. Mostly she gets A+ instead of just A. She is that smart. She's afraid that we'll miss studying in New York.

I tried to set her straight. I told Lindsay that even though the test was important, there was NO WAY she could cancel her amazing birthday celebration. OMG! The 4 of us have never ever gone to NYC together even though it's just $1/2$ hour away. This is one of those lifetime opportunities. And besides, we could study on the train, right?

But even when I begged, Lindsay still seemed unsure. I wanted to scream. What's her dilemma?

Rude Awakening: This is waaaaay more than just a birthday. It is a medical emergency. We practically need to take CPR to keep the life in Lindsay's party.

Madison hit SAVE.

Her laptop buzzed as it saved the file, and she tapped her fingers nervously on the desktop, waiting for the final "you're all set!" beep. She always hated it when her computer went *ding* in the middle of the quiet library. Madison did not like anything that drew unnecessary attention to her, especially when she was busy writing in her files.

But someone had heard the *ding*. Out of the corner of her eye, she caught a glimpse of red sweater. The person wearing the sweater strolled toward Madison like a secret-service agent, arms pressed tight against his sides, face pinched with concern. It was Hart, but Madison had never seen him looking so serious. Next to Hart, walking just as fast, was Egg. He looked serious, too.

They didn't make a huge fuss but sat down in chairs on either side of Madison and began talking as if they had been sequestered in some kind of interrogation room. Madison felt as though she were in the hot seat—and not just because of the boys' battery of questions. Madison was hot because her face felt flushed. Her skin prickled.

She stared again absentmindedly at her crush. As his lips moved she wondered (as she often wondered) whether or not Hart was the kind of guy who would like the flavor of Madison's lip gloss.

"What are you doing up here?" Madison asked the boys.

"We're looking for you," Egg joked.

Madison rolled her eyes.

"Seriously, we were," Hart said.

Madison neatly closed the laptop cover and crossed her arms. "What for?" she asked.

"Yo, I have to boogie," Egg announced, like a circus ringmaster, gesturing to the right and left and finally slinging his bag over his back with a loud swoosh. "Hockey later, dude?" he asked Hart.

Hart nodded. "Later," he said.

Madison was beginning to get the distinct impression that something was going on between the two friends. Sometimes they didn't use actual words, but seemed to communicate in shorthand. As Egg walked away, Madison turned to Hart. There was a glint in his eye, but he didn't speak. He just stared.

"Um . . . Hart," Madison said. "I'm sorry about the other day. About the tongue, I mean."

Hart gave Madison a blank stare. "The tongue? Huh? What are you talking about?"

Madison's throat muscles clenched.

"Um . . . nothing . . . I guess . . ." She wanted to run, but she pasted a smile on her lips instead. He obviously had forgotten all about that moment at the end of class.

"Hey," Hart said, clearing his throat. "Are you working on the science homework or studying for those stupid standardized tests?"

"Neither," Madison admitted with a sigh. "I was writing in my online journal. I keep these computer files. . . ."

"Files?" Hart repeated. "What's in the files?"

Madison thought about saying, "Duh! What do you think? All of my daydreams about you, dork!" But she didn't say any of that.

"Well," Madison continued aloud. "I keep track of all my feelings and ideas and . . . oh, you know. I can't believe I'm telling you this. I mean, you can't possibly care about my files or my feelings or anything. . . ."

"Huh?" Hart said, taking a deep breath. Madison

could see his Adam's apple move in a jerky gulp. "Sure I care. I'm your friend."

"Oh," Madison replied. *Friend?*

There was a moment of silence. Both tongues were tied—tight.

Madison giggled nervously.

Then Hart giggled.

"Finnster, can I ask you something?"

Madison grabbed the table and pushed back in her seat so that she was balancing on the back two legs of the chair. "Sure," she said, coolly kicking her legs out and pinching the table edge so she didn't tip all the way back.

"Finnster, do you remember . . . when I asked you out to the movies with everyone?" Hart asked really fast.

Madison closed her eyes and then opened them again, as if she were blinking in slow motion.

"I remember," Madison said expectantly.

Yes, this really was Hart Jones. Yes, she really was Madison Finn. Yes, he really *had* just said that.

"I totally remember," Madison said.

"Well . . . do you want to do that again sometime, maybe . . . for real?"

"Yeah," Madison said, still trying to act cool while her insides were doing loops on an imaginary roller coaster.

Hart exhaled. His shoulders dipped down.

"I was thinking. . . ." He spoke very slowly.

Madison could tell that he was nervous. He didn't want to mess this up.

"I was thinking that we could go to the mall on Saturday," Hart said.

"Wow," Madison said.

"They have this car show, and I was thinking that you and me, I mean, you and I, could go to this car show. . . ."

"Car show?" Madison made a funny face.

"Or not. Scratch that. We don't have to go to the car show," Hart cried. "That was just a dumb guy idea. Egg told me to say that."

Madison pushed the chair upright again. There was no leaning back now. She was already off balance enough. She fiddled with the hem of her sweater.

Egg told me to say that.

So, Egg knew about what Hart was planning to do?

"Forget I said car show. That was wicked lame. Let's go to the stores or something else that you want to do. Just hang. Play videos. Whatever. My dad said there's this new take-out Italian restaurant in the Food Court called Napolis or something. He told me what I could order. We could go there, I guess, right?"

"I guess."

"Ever eaten calamari? It's squid."

Madison chuckled. "Squid?" she said.

Hart nodded. "Gross, huh?"

They both burst into laughter. Madison clapped her hand over her mouth so that Mr. Books, the librarian, wouldn't chase her out of the library with one of his "silence at all times" lectures.

Hart kept right on laughing. Even his eyes were grinning. Had Madison ever seen him look this happy? Had she ever been this happy? She wished that someone could take a photograph to prove that it really was happening.

Aimee, Fiona, and Lindsay wouldn't believe it.

"What about a movie?" Madison asked.

"If you want to go to a movie, I'd have to ask my dad for permission. He said he'd come along as a chaperone, unless you wanted to ask your mom to drive us . . . and I heard that on Saturdays the mall is starting this new concert series."

"Oh, no," Madison said, her expression changing from a smile to a frown. "Saturday? This Saturday?"

"What's wrong with Saturday?" Hart asked.

"I can't go," Madison said. She hung her head.

"Huh?"

"I can't go," Madison repeated. "I can't go this Saturday."

Hart's face froze. Madison wasn't sure what to say next.

"You really can't go?" Hart asked.

"I can explain," Madison said. But she didn't know what else to say. "There's this party. . . ."

"Yeah, sure," Hart said. "That's cool. I under-stand."

Although the library was perfectly quiet, Madison heard the imaginary sound of screeching brakes. She nervously grabbed at her neck. If it had been a teen movie, she would have leaped into his arms and nuzzled *his* neck.

But this was no movie.

"Um . . . what about . . . well . . . can we do it *next* weekend instead of this weekend?" Madison asked.

"No, I can't," Hart shrugged. "My dad is only free this weekend, which is why I asked you for that day. I have hockey games every weekend for the rest of the winter, pretty much."

"Oh," Madison said dumbly.

"So you can't go? Is that what you're saying?"

"Not exactly . . . well, yes . . ." Madison could hardly speak.

"Gee, I guess I should go now," Hart said. His shoulders had slumped again.

"Wait!" Madison cried. "Don't be weird, Hart, please. I want to go out with you. But I just can't do it then."

"No, that's cool. I understand. Totally," Hart said.

"No, you don't," Madison said.

"I don't?"

"What I mean is . . ."

"Forget about it. We can talk later," Hart said.

"Later," Madison repeated. "You can't talk now?"

"Nah," Hart mumbled. "I have a lot of really, really important stuff to do."

"Oh," Madison said. "You do?"

She watched him pick up his bag and turn solemnly toward the library door and then, taking giant steps, disappear into the hallway without once looking back at Madison.

Stunned, Madison sat back down in front of her laptop and idly hit SAVE again just to make sure that her previous file was still there.

It was.

But something else was missing.

A little piece of her heart had just left the library.

"Maddie, you have to stop crying," Fiona said as she rubbed Madison's back. "It's a good thing that happened. Not a bad thing."

Aimee and Lindsay sat close by. The four friends were hanging out on the wall outside school, waiting to catch a glimpse of Hart Jones. But it looked as though he—and all of his other friends—had most definitely left the building.

"I blew it," Madison said, sniffling.

"You did not blow it," Aimee reassured her friend. "He blew it."

"What?" Madison wiped her cheeks but the tears kept coming. "It wasn't his fault I couldn't say the right thing."

45

"Well, he didn't have to walk away, either," Aimee said.

Fiona groaned. "Aim, Hart didn't walk. He ran. He was mortified. Madison rejected him."

"I didn't reject him!" Madison cried.

"You did," Aimee said.

"I did not!"

"That's not how Hart sees it," Lindsay said.

"Whose side are you guys on?" Madison asked.

"Why didn't you just tell him the truth about Lindsay's birthday party?" Fiona asked.

Madison shrugged. "I don't know. I couldn't speak. All the wrong things kept coming out of my mouth."

"Yeah, well . . . Maybe you did blow it," Aimee said.

"Aim!" Fiona gave Aimee a light punch in the shoulder. "You're meaner than Poison Ivy!"

Madison cracked a small smile. "I appreciate your trying to help," she said.

"Why don't we just call him or E him and tell him the truth? He'll understand," Lindsay suggested. She always opted for a practical solution.

"I guess you're right," Madison said. "But what if he doesn't understand or forgive me? What if that was my one and only chance to finally get Hart Jones to ask me on a date and I totally ruined it?"

"Maddie, the two of you are meant to be together," Fiona said.

"Hart will ask you out again," Lindsay said. "Eventually."

"Yeah," Madison agreed. "Eventually. To him that means another year of waiting and flirting and—aargh!—I'll be a senior in high school before we ever go out for real. If I make it that far."

Fiona, Aimee, and Lindsay threw their arms around Madison.

"You'll always have us," they all said practically at the same time, their voices muffled as they squeezed together.

Madison knew it was true, but for some reason a friend hug didn't feel quite the same as a Hart hug. She couldn't get Hart's face out of her thoughts. She saw herself reflected in his happy, dancing eyes.

It had only been an hour. She missed him.

Her friends began talking among themselves about the standardized test. Aimee had an old textbook to share while they studied, and they flipped through the long chapters. But Madison couldn't study. Not now.

Madison scanned the parking lot and the area in front of the school building, hoping that maybe Hart would pop out from behind a tree and rush over toward her. That was the way it would have worked on a sitcom. That was how she'd have written the happy ending to a play.

A cluster of clouds drifted by, taking on different

shapes. Madison wanted to be swallowed whole by the sky. She wanted to take back the day.

Lindsay wasn't the only one with a major dilemma. Madison had one of her own.

What was more important: a best friend's birthday party or a real date with the one boy she had ever loved?

Chapter 5

Madison moved her cursor across the home page of the bigfishbowl.com Web site. She checked the site's main bulletin board for new postings. Lately, the Webmaster had been adding a lot of graphics and features to the site, and Madison liked to keep on top of the changes.

Egg always challenged Madison to see if she knew as much as he did about what was on the site. He was obnoxious about it, but of course he was obnoxious about *everything*. He'd been competing with Madison since they had been young. It was practically like having a brother, Madison thought. But unlike Fiona, who had one annoying twin brother named Chet, and Aimee, who had four annoying brothers named Roger, Billy, Dean, and Doug, Madison didn't have to share toys or fight for the remote control. She wouldn't have to *see* Egg if she didn't want to.

Madison had to reenter her password to enter the Members Only area. Madison always wondered what that meant, since anyone could be a member. It was free. The site recommended that users change their passwords every few weeks for security purposes. Madison spelled out her latest:

IHEARTHART

She laughed to herself. It was such a ridiculous password (so-o-o-o-o ridiculous!) and yet she loved it all the same—even now.

The screen buzzed and glowed a shade of lime green. She clicked her keypad to enter the Bloggerfishbowl section. This was the fastest growing area. The screen flashed a few times as the blogger welcome greeting popped up.

Welcome to BLOGGERFISHBOWL!

Although she didn't have a blog of her own, Madison visited to check out her keypal Bigwheels's blog. She scrolled down the list of bloggers until she came across the right one.

Don't Ask: The Whole Truth
A blog by Vicki (aka Bigwheels)

Madison selected the blog name and clicked. A separate screen opened with her online friend's latest entry.

School is a big drag & I haven't been feeling right these days. First off my BFF Lainie has been out sick and that bums me out when she's not around to talk :>(The other big news is that the doctors keep changing the diagnosis on my little bro. Mom always tells me these things about his autism but I forget most of it. All I know is that he looks like he's staring into space sometimes and I never know when he's going to throw his toys around. It's weird. My mom spends most of the time trying to keep him away from my younger sister. He almost pushed her down the basement stairs by accident. But she's ok. N e way, M & D say I need to try to understand more but the thing is I am trying--hard. Maybe I need to try harder. I made a list of all the Web sites where I can

get info. One very, VERY good
thing this week is that I aced my
American history report (finally)
and I got a really good score on
the standardized test they had in
our district. So many people failed
or did really badly. AND I saved
up some money I got babysitting 2
get this amazing purple sweater
set that makes me look skinny. I
think I will wear it to the school
dance if Reggie asks me. I just
need a pair of earrings 2 go
w/it. BLOGYL!

Madison opened a new window on her screen
and up popped her e-mailbox. She needed to talk to
Bigwheels. There was so much going on in both their
worlds.

But before she could hit NEW MAIL, her laptop
beeped. An Insta-Message appeared in another new
window on the screen.

```
<Bigwheels>: ur online--that is 22C
<MadFinn>: I was just reading yr
    blog!!!!
<Bigwheels>: it's kind of lame,
    right?
<MadFinn>: nope it's gr8
<Bigwheels>: My mom doesn't like
```

it. she told me I shouldn't write
so much personal stuff so I was
thinking I would maybe stop
writing online and just keep a
journal 4 myself what do u think?
mom is worried about internet
stalkers. She saw some story on
the news

<MadFinn>: I know my dad & mom
worry 2 b/c I do so much on the
computer but I try 2 be careful

<Bigwheels>: I told mom that no one
probably reads my dumb blog
anyhow

<MadFinn>: Except me :>*

<Bigwheels>: got yr e-mail BTW

<MadFinn>: OMG total catastrophe
since I wrote that

<Bigwheels>: WHA?

<MadFinn>: Hart asked me on a date

<Bigwheels>: awesome WOW

<MadFinn>: BUT there's a but

<Bigwheels>: <:-Z what?

<MadFinn>: I had 2 say NO

<Bigwheels>: Y?

Madison explained to Bigwheels about the party
with Lindsay in New York and how all her BFFs were
going to be there and how she had made a decision
to tell Hart no because of the birthday bash.

<Bigwheels>: IGI b/c friends ALWAYS
   should come first
<MadFinn>: u think? I didn't make a
   mistake???
<Bigwheels>: No way! FCF!
<MadFinn>: thanks u always give good
   advice
<Bigwheels>: go out w/hart another
   time
<MadFinn>: IF he asks me
<Bigwheels>: he will (:9
<MadFinn>: VVF
<Bigwheels>: I have 2 go soon
   I'm @ school but I have class
   and my mom is picking me up
   early we have another appt.
   w/Eddie's doctors and she likes
   it when I come she says he
   always is happier when i'm
   there
<MadFinn>: that's good right?
<Bigwheels>: yeah I guess it's just
   hard when I wanna do something
   else u know?
<MadFinn>: u mean like go out
   w/Lainie
<Bigwheels>: Yup
<MadFinn>: I better go 2 then
   HOMEWORK
<Bigwheels>: Blahblahblah
<MadFinn>: LYLAS online!

```
<Bigwheels>: ditto
<MadFinn>: *poof*
```

"Are you packed yet?" Mom shouted upstairs. Madison snapped her laptop shut and raced over to the door.

"Not yet!" Madison called back.

Mom appeared at the bottom of the stairs with Phin in her arms. She was scratching the scruff of his neck, and he loved it. He stretched his furry little neck to the side and let out a low doggy moan.

"Maddie, I'm still a little nervous about your being in the city by yourself," Mom said with a serious look.

Madison laughed. "Mom, you know we'll be fine."

"I know, I know," Mom said.

Madison made a confused face. "So what do I pack?"

"Maddie! Don't make it such a production! It's only two nights. Bring your nice pants, a sweater, a couple of T-shirts, your boots, in case the weather changes. I heard it might rain tomorrow."

"Rain?" Madison grimaced. "Oh, no. Then we won't be able to walk around."

"You can still walk. Just bring your rain gear and that yellow pocket umbrella in the hall closet."

"I guess," Madison grumbled. As she turned back

toward her room, Phinnie leaped from Mom's arms and scooted up the stairs.

"It's your turn to walk the dog tonight. Don't forget," Mom said.

Madison's head raced. She had a lot to do before school tomorrow and no time to do it. And she hadn't even thought much about studying for the standardized test. She assumed that Lindsay would bring study materials along on the weekend in the city. Even if they didn't have much time to look over vocabulary and math problems and whatever else was going to be on the test, Lindsay would take comfort in the fact that she had all of her study guides close at hand.

Luckily, the packing went quicker than quick. She stuffed two different dress-up tops and skirts into the bag just in case she needed options. Aimee was always saying that the key to being a fashion diva was options, which was funny, considering the fact that sometimes Aimee would wear the same ballet tights and shoes for four days in a row.

Madison had no idea what kind of special restaurant Lindsay's Aunt Mimi would be taking them to, but she assumed it would be fancy-schmancy. That was what Madison's Gramma Helen always called places where they had a special waiter just for pouring water and refilling the bread basket, and at least three different forks per place setting. With this in mind, Madison packed a couple of pairs of earrings, including a moonstone pair that matched her favorite moonstone ring, the one that Dad had bought her.

Dad liked to buy Madison presents for no reason. He called them "little kisses, all wrapped up." Sometimes when they were out together, he would stop in front of a jewelry store and make Madison choose the top five things she would have purchased if she had been a multimillionaire. They always played games like that when they shopped. And without fail (and just as a joke) Madison would select the most expensive item—for example, a diamond necklace. Of course, Madison didn't really like flashy pieces like that. She liked jewelry that looked as though it told a story: necklaces with lots of beads, or earrings with oddly shaped opalescent stones.

This week, with the trip into the city for Lindsay's party, Madison would be missing her weekend visit with Dad. She'd almost forgotten, because she had been so focused on missing the date with Hart. Dad would have to wait, just like her crush. Madison couldn't ever remember having so many choices—and being less sure of which was the right one.

But the party was the number-one pick. And tomorrow after school, Madison, Aimee, Fiona, and Lindsay would be driven to the train station by Lindsay's mother. They would board the four o'clock train into New York City, loaded down with duffel bags and backpacks, their heads filled with big ideas about skyscrapers and shopping.

Madison zipped her suitcase shut and clapped her hands to get Phinnie's attention. At last, she was ready to walk the dog.

She was ready for *anything*.

Chapter 6

Before the renovation, the elevator of the Far Hills train station had been out of order, on and off, for at least a year. There was only one small ticket window and one crabby ticket agent. Madison had been there a few times to take trains into the city with Mom or Dad or her stepmother, Stephanie. She remembered a funny smell coming from the waiting area, where the benches were covered with old newspapers and graffiti.

But today, as the girls arrived at the station, there was a completely different sight to behold. Everything gleamed. The elevator had been overhauled and the benches replaced. The lone ticket agent had been replaced, too, by three shiny machines where tickets could be purchased automatically.

Madison took the renovation as a good omen for the weekend. She believed that the sight of the bright stairs and seats inside the station meant one thing: she had made the correct decision about Lindsay's party. Hart could wait. Dad could wait. She was doing the one thing that couldn't wait—and that she couldn't possibly miss. As Bigwheels said, FCF (friends come first)!

"I can't believe this place." Madison's eyes widened as the group ambled into the main part of the station.

But no one else was particularly surprised. Madison was the only one who hadn't taken the train into the city lately. Aimee often took the train into New York to see a ballet performance and meet up with one of her friends from ballet camp. Fiona and Chet sometimes traveled into Manhattan with their dad. And Lindsay was always shuttling back and forth into the city to see Aunt Mimi or to dine with one of her parents at some trendy spot.

Madison headed for the ticket machine, but Lindsay grabbed her arm.

"We can chill out until the train comes. I already have our tickets," Lindsay announced.

"You are such a rock star," Aimee said. "This is like some kind of glam weekend, with all expenses paid, like we won a game show."

60

Lindsay laughed. "You think?"

"Yeah," Madison added, heaving her too-heavy bag over her shoulder. "Thanks, Lindsay—for everything."

"Why did you bring such a big bag, Maddie?" Fiona asked when she spotted Madison heaving the overstuffed duffel.

Madison shrugged. "I don't know. Because I couldn't pick just one thing to wear?"

"Are you feeling fashion-challenged *again*?" Aimee cracked. "Maddie, you should go on one of those makeover shows."

"I wish. They don't have them for kids our age," Madison moaned.

"They don't?" Fiona asked. She paused thoughtfully. "I don't know why you guys obsess about clothes. Who cares what we wear, as long as we have fun?"

"Are you kidding?" Aimee exclaimed. "Clothes are key."

"No, I think Fiona's probably right," Madison said with a wide smile. It had seemed easier to bring everything along rather than face the prospect of getting caught without the right color top or the right pair of shoes. But after hearing Fiona speak, Madison wished that she could dump half her bag right there on the ground and return to her closet for a re-pack. If only there were a rewind button for life.

61

"What about you, Lindsay?" Fiona asked.

"I didn't bring that many clothes, but I *did* bring books for that test on Monday," Lindsay said.

"I *knew* you would bring something to study!" Aimee said.

Madison chuckled. "Me, too."

"Me three," Fiona said. "Or at least I was hoping you would. I'm worried about spending all weekend shopping and not studying. Um . . . is anyone else worried?"

Madison shrugged, but Lindsay nodded emphatically. "Are you kidding? I'm so-o-o-o worried. Aunt Mimi told me that I can't study on my birthday. But we can find the time. I know it."

"Come on. I refuse to worry about something I don't even *get*," Aimee said. "There are only three things I worry about: ballet recitals, my brothers throwing me in the pool in the summer, and Ben Buckley liking me." She giggled out loud, and her friends giggled, too.

"Ben?" Fiona exclaimed.

"Gee, you haven't talked about Ben in a while," Lindsay said.

Madison rolled her eyes. "Don't encourage her."

Madison always found it strange that Aimee, who was definitely one of the prettiest girls in the class, didn't go for any of the most popular—or

62

cutest—boys. Instead, Aimee decided to like one of the shyest—and smartest—kids in the seventh grade, Benjamin Buckley III.

"Yeah, too bad Ben isn't here," Madison quipped. "Then he could help us study for the test. Mr. IQ could take one of these tests with his eyes shut."

The train was due in the station in only a few minutes, so the girls dragged their stuff out onto the platform to wait. The air was brisk. Everyone bundled up in scarves and gloves or shoved their hands into their pockets. Madison inhaled deeply. She loved the way cold air felt when she breathed it into her lungs. It was almost minty.

Across the platform, the girls watched as a train-load of people disembarked. They had come from the direction of the city, and many of them carried briefcases and laptop computers. Madison smiled at the thought that she had her own laptop tucked neatly inside her orange bag.

A loud whistle blew, and the girls jumped.

North of where they stood, the bright white lights of a train could be seen in the distance. A low clattering grew louder as the train approached.

"I can't believe we're going to the city together," Lindsay said excitedly.

The four friends bobbed up and down, partly from excitement and partly because they were getting cold.

"I can't believe we didn't do this sooner," Aimee said.

As soon as the train stopped, the doors opened with a loud ping. Madison and the others quickly shuffled inside. Although it was an express train, there were many seats open. Lindsay found two double seats facing each other for the four of them. They placed their bags in the open rack above the seats, hauling them up carefully one by one so nothing would crash to the floor during the ride.

Madison settled into her leather-upholstered seat near the window just as the train lurched and started back on its route. As she leaned close to the window, she could feel the cold through the glass. Outside, rows of trees lined the tracks. The trees were bare, and the houses behind them were visible. Madison could see inside some of the kitchens and bedrooms as the train rushed past.

Lindsay pulled out three small, flat, rectangular packages from her knapsack and handed them to the other girls.

"What is this?" Fiona asked.

"Something silly," Lindsay said, eyes twinkling.

"Get out of here!" Aimee said. "What *is* this?"

Madison shook her little package. "It doesn't rattle or anything. Hmmm . . ."

Lindsay tilted her head to one side. "Well, it's not anything big. Aunt Mimi had this idea, since we're together all weekend. Oh, just open it."

Madison, Aimee, and Fiona ripped at the wrapping paper at the same time. Fiona was the first to reveal the gift. Inside each package was a laminated card marked LINDSAY'S BIRTHDAY PASS, with a photo of the recipient at the center. Each pass was attached to a long pink glitter cord, recalling the pink glitter on the last-minute invitations. On the back was a list of interesting things: Frrrozen hot chocolate, constellations, and fashion shows.

"Huh?" Aimee said, trying to figure out what exactly it was all supposed to mean.

Lindsay wrinkled her nose. "It was Aunt Mimi's idea. She made me send her photos of each of you, and she had someone make these up. Please don't laugh. You can throw it out if you want."

"Throw it out? What are you talking about?" Aimee declared. "It's like a backstage pass. This is totally cool."

Madison nodded. "Cooler than cool."

"What an incredible weekend," Fiona said. "Special passes? Where are we going to go?"

"I told you. I'm not sure," Lindsay said.

When the conductor passed through the train car to collect the fares, Lindsay reached into her bag for the tickets.

Fiona jokingly held up her party pass and smiled.

"Excuse me, ma'am, but I think these passes

should be good enough to get us to New York, right?"

The conductor squinted and tried to read Fiona's pass. "Huh? What is this thing? I don't accept these. Where is your ticket?"

Fiona shook her head and stifled a laugh. "It was . . . um . . . just a joke," she mumbled. But the conductor didn't think much of Fiona's joke. She took their *real* tickets and moved along to the next car.

Madison, Aimee, Lindsay, and Fiona burst into laughter as soon as she was out of earshot.

Thweeeeeeeeeeeeek!

The train's brakes made a loud, squeaking noise as the train slid past the Harlem-125th Street station and headed underground toward the heart of New York City. The interior was thrust into darkness as the train chugged into Grand Central.

"Party pass?" Lindsay asked aloud in the dark. The girls tried their hardest to keep themselves from cracking up *again*, but by now it was useless. One laugh led to another, and soon it was an avalanche of giggles. People were actually staring. Madison was cracking up so hard she needed to pee.

When the train finally pulled into Grand Central for the last stop—their stop—the girls slowly retrieved their duffel bags and backpacks. A nice gentleman helped the girls lift the bags back onto the floor so they didn't lose their balance and drop everything. By the time they had all of their stuff in order, they were the last four people to exit the train.

They walked up a long ramp and then up a flight of stairs toward the interior of the station. Lindsay directed everyone through two passageways, past a coffee bar and a newsstand, and the girls entered the main part of Grand Central. The foursome narrowly missed bumping into a cluster of kids who weren't paying attention. Fiona nearly collided with a kiosk. A businessman wearing a phone headset sideswiped Madison with his briefcase and didn't even look back.

But none of that mattered. They were there—at last.

Madison threw her head back and gasped. Although she had, in fact, seen the Grand Central Station ceiling a dozen times—or more—it never failed to awe her. As they walked toward the center of the main room of the station, Madison and the others huddled together and stared up at the blue-green ceiling decorated with gold stars. Dusky light streamed in through windows around the top of the room, through wide panes of glass that had been there for more than a century.

The buzz of people racing across the vast room invigorated all four girls. They couldn't stop oohing and aahing as they spun around, eyes darting from the posh restaurant up on the second level to the armed security guards standing at attention by the exit doors. Aimee spotted someone famous, or at least she thought she did, but after a few expectant moments Lindsay (who was always seriously in the know) burst her bubble. Aimee literally had stars in her eyes—or at least she wished she did.

Madison's head hummed with all the noise. Her bags felt heavy but she didn't mind. Glancing around, she caught the eye of a young boy who seemed to be checking her out. She did a double take. Hart!

Of course it wasn't the real Hart, but someone who looked exactly like him.

"Aunt Mimi!" Lindsay cried suddenly. She raced toward the large information booth at the center of the room. Atop the booth was a four-sided clock. Madison could see from the ornate brass hands of the clock that it was nearly four-thirty.

"Lindsay!" Aunt Mimi screeched at the top of her lungs. "Girls!" she added, arms flailing under a patchwork cape.

Lindsay ran over for a hug. Madison, Aimee, and Fiona straggled behind with their bags.

"Good ride?" Aunt Mimi asked, her voice lilting.

Up close, Madison saw Mimi's charcoal eyeliner and scarlet lipstick. Her makeup accentuated her perfect cheekbones and eyelashes—like those of a magazine cover model, Madison thought. For some reason she had imagined Lindsay's wacky aunt Mimi as someone older, with silver hair and lots of wrinkles. But this Mimi teetered on a pair of three-inch-high black heels and wore a brown fur cap with little fur pom-poms like the kind Madison saw in fashion magazines. Everything about Lindsay's aunt was unexpected.

"Are you four tired? Hungry? Bored? All of the above?" Aunt Mimi asked.

Aimee, Fiona, and Madison laughed out loud at Aunt Mimi's stand-up-comedy delivery. Lindsay was amused, too, although she was clearly used to the act.

"Aunt Mimi, I told everyone that we'd go to your place first. That way we can dump our stuff," Lindsay said.

"Abso-tootly!" Mimi cried as she readjusted her pom-poms. "Do you have your passes?" she asked with a wink.

Lindsay groaned. "Aunt Mimi . . ."

"I have mine!" Fiona said as she pulled it out of her pocket.

Aimee produced her pass, too, with a wide smile. "We decided these were the coolest things on the planet," she said to Aunt Mimi. "So . . . where are you taking us?"

"Hmmm," Aunt Mimi said thoughtfully. "Every-where I can possibly take you in two short days. Sound good?"

Aimee nodded.

69

Aunt Mimi craned her neck and glanced at the information-booth clock. "Well then, if we're going everywhere, we've got no time to lose!" she declared, throwing her shoulders back.

"No time!" Fiona and Aimee said simultaneously.

"I told you that Aunt Mimi is crazy, but she's fun," Lindsay whispered. "I promise."

Madison lifted her two bags and steadied herself. It felt as if the floor were moving. Even though they had only been standing there a few minutes, the crowd of people rushing to their trains seemed to have grown twofold around them. Rush-hour traffic on a Friday·in Grand Central Station made this one of the busiest places on earth.

Cell phones beeped with annoying ring tones. The loudspeaker blared. But for some strange reason Madison didn't feel swallowed up by the people elbowing their way around her· and her friends where they stood, or by the very loud shuffling and pounding as people made their way from one side of the room to the other. Madison felt bigger than all of it, bigger than the information-booth clock, bigger than the starry sky that was painted on the ceiling.

"To the subway!" Aunt Mimi announced with a loud flourish, as if she were waving a magic wand.

Bags in hand and on backs, Madison and the others followed their leader to the Number Six subway train, gliding across the station's marble floor together toward the great unknown.

Or at least toward the upper east side of Manhattan.

Chapter 7

"I haven't been on the subway in so long," Madison announced. Her friends didn't hear her. They were busy pushing their way through the turnstiles.

Down a tiled corridor, the train was just pulling in with a whoosh of cold underground air.

"Let's dash!" Aunt Mimi called out as she ran for the train.

The girls scrambled into the subway car. Fiona almost lost her purse, but Aimee grabbed it in the nick of time. Getting used to the pace of the city was tricky. People crowded in around them.

Madison and Lindsay sat down in two free seats near one of the doors. Aimee, Fiona, and Aunt Mimi checked out the illuminated subway map overhead.

"What do you think so far?" Lindsay asked.

"Your aunt is amazing," Madison said.

Lindsay nodded. "I know. But I don't know how she and my mom could possibly be sisters."

"Your mom is nice, too," Madison said.

"Yeah, but she isn't cool. Not like Aunt Mimi."

"Are any moms truly cool?" Madison asked with a laugh.

"Your mom is," Lindsay answered. "She makes movies. She travels all over the world."

"But she doesn't wear fur hats or capes," Madison said.

From across the subway car, Aunt Mimi shot the girls a look. "Are you two conspiring?"

Lindsay laughed. "Of course."

The subway doors finally closed, and the train headed uptown. At one stop, some people speaking Spanish got off, and Aimee and Fiona slid into their seats, across from Madison and Lindsay. Aunt Mimi stood between the girls, hanging onto the silver bars as the train chugged along, as if she were balancing on an exercise machine. With her high heels, Aunt Mimi towered over them all.

They arrived at their station and scooted up the escalator to the street level. Aunt Mimi wanted to walk the rest of the way to her apartment. It was only a few more blocks uptown.

When the girls exited the subway station, traffic was at a standstill. Yellow cabs honked loudly. A bus exhaled gritty exhaust in front of them. Aunt Mimi coughed.

"How lovely," Aunt Mimi sputtered. "Welcome to New York."

They crossed the street and strolled past a clothing store with a flashy CHRISTMAS AND HANUKKAH ARE COMING! sign; a restaurant advertising special prix fixe menus and little tables set with candles; and several shops selling T-shirts and newspapers out in front. It was a metropolitan obstacle course, with Aunt Mimi leading the way. Madison, Aimee, Fiona, and Lindsay clung to their bags and moved in a pack so they would not get separated.

"I love the city," Aimee declared as they passed one store. "Look at this!"

The store window displayed a ballerina dressed in tulle. Of all the stores in New York, Aimee had found the one with ballet clothes. Aunt Mimi suggested that they go inside the store for a look.

Aunt Mimi and Aimee headed for a sale rack. Fiona followed them, leaving Madison and Lindsay to guard the luggage at the front of the store.

"So, when's your mom coming?" Madison asked Lindsay.

Lindsay shrugged. "Later, I guess. She said she would call. I don't know about my dad, though. He hasn't called me back yet today."

"But he's coming, right?" Madison asked.

"I don't know," Lindsay said. "I hope."

Madison knew how hard things had been for Lindsay lately. Everyone knew the basics: Lindsay's parents were in the process of splitting up. But that was all anyone knew. Lindsay hardly ever mentioned her family problems, not even when she was confiding in Madison via e-mail or near the lockers at school.

Aimee decided to buy a pink leotard with flowers around the neck, because it was on sale.

"You girls have been here for five minutes, and you're already shopping!" Aunt Mimi laughed. "What do you say we head for home now?"

Four blocks later, they arrived at Aunt Mimi's apartment building. It had metal, mirrored windows and a gigantic lobby filled with abstract art and a fountain made of colored glass.

"'Evening, Miss Frost," the doorman said, tipping his hat. He stood behind an enormous marble desk surrounded by video monitors and buttons. "How are you tonight?"

"I'm fabulous, George. I've got my niece and her friends for the weekend."

George grinned. "Can I take your bags up?"

Aunt Mimi waved him off. "We've lugged them for blocks," she said. "We can make the elevator. Thank you."

George tipped his hat again. "Ladies . . ." he said as Lindsay and her friends passed by. Aunt Mimi led everyone to the bank of elevators. Once inside the wood-paneled elevator car, she pulled out a small key and pushed it into the control panel.

"What was that?" Aimee asked aloud.

"She has a special key for her floor," Lindsay explained.

"She has a whole floor?" Madison asked.

"Indeed I do," Aunt Mimi said.

"Wow," Fiona said. "That's a lot of rooms."

"She has one room just for clothes," Lindsay whispered. "And it's bigger than my bedroom at home."

"It is not!" Aunt Mimi let out a laugh. "Lindsay, it's just a closet. And you kids are welcome to try on anything and borrow anything this weekend, by the way. My home is your home."

Madison, Aimee, and Fiona giggled as the elevator climbed all the way up, to the penthouse level, finally opening onto a wide hallway with mosaic tiles on the floor. They saw a giant wooden door with a knocker carved like a lion's head.

Aunt Mimi punched a few keys on the automatic-alarm keypad and turned the front doorknob.

The girls gasped. It was like a movie set inside.

Everyone froze in their steps, but Lindsay ran inside without making a big fuss. "Don't just stand there. Come on, everyone," she said.

The ceilings were at least twenty feet high, Madison thought as they wandered inside and placed their stuff along one wall.

Aunt Mimi flung her cape onto one of the four sofas in the living room. Or was it the living room? Madison could see out of the corner of her eye that there were at least four or five other rooms connected to this one—and they all looked like living rooms.

"Make yourselves comfy," Aunt Mimi said.

Just outside the apartment, the sun was setting, and the room was filled with a golden-orange light. Madison, Aimee, Fiona, and Lindsay each collapsed onto her own sofa. Aunt Mimi handed Aimee a cell phone so that she—and the other girls—could call home to let their mothers know they had arrived safely.

Lindsay had to call her mom, too. She paced around the room as they talked for about five minutes. She seemed fine when she was talking, but as soon as she got off the phone her face turned blank.

"What's the matter?" Fiona asked.

"Lindsay, are you okay?" Aimee asked.

"Everything is fine, which means everything is not fine," Lindsay remarked. "It's the same as usual."

Her eyes filled up. A tear trickled down one cheek.

"Lindsay, don't cry," Madison said.

Aunt Mimi put an arm around Lindsay's shoulder. "My darling Lindsay, things always have a way of working out."

"That's what everyone says," Lindsay cried. "Um . . ."

She ran into the other room.

For a moment, no one said a word. Then Aunt Mimi excused herself and followed Lindsay into one of the rooms in the back. As soon as the two had disappeared, Madison, Aimee, and Fiona began to whisper.

"What do you think is wrong?" Fiona asked.

"You know," Aimee said.

"I'm worried," Madison said.

"Can you believe this apartment?" Aimee said suddenly. "It's more like a castle."

"You could fit our whole house inside here," Fiona said.

"I hope she's okay," Madison said with concern.

"I think Lindsay is just worked up because this is a big weekend," Aimee said matter-of-factly. "And she misses her mom and dad, but they'll be here. No worries."

Madison gave Aimee a funny look.

"Plus, it's a really big deal to turn thirteen," Fiona said.

Madison shook her head. What were they talking about? Didn't they understand anything?

Madison understood. She knew *exactly* why Lindsay was upset, or at least she thought she did.

Just then, Aunt Mimi reappeared at a side door, with Lindsay in tow.

"Sorry, guys," Lindsay said. "I just lost it for a minute. My mom said she would be late tomorrow, and I really wanted her to come shopping with us. That's all. I didn't mean to get so freaked."

"I'm glad you feel better," Fiona said.

Aunt Mimi threw her arms into the air. "Why don't you four come into the kitchen? I've prepared a sleepover feast—and you are invited."

Lindsay laughed with relief. "Aunt Mimi is an awesome cook," she said. "She made four-cheese macaroni and grilled chicken kebabs and salad and all my favorites."

"Yum," Fiona said, rubbing her belly for effect. Of course Fiona would find those foods appealing. She would eat anything, except bananas and most fruit.

The girls entered the kitchen and immediately began to pick at the assortment of food on the countertop.

"Thanks for making a vegetarian-friendly dinner," Aimee said.

"Sometimes I feel like a rabbit, I love salad so much," Lindsay said. "And Aunt Mimi makes the best rice-vinegar dressing." She reached into the salad bowl, then popped a carrot stick into her mouth.

"Aunt Mimi, is there anything you can't do?" Madison asked.

"Well, I can't be thirteen again," Aunt Mimi said sweetly. "You four have everything ahead of you . . . everything to look forward to."

"I guess," Aimee said, grabbing a tortilla chip from a large ceramic bowl.

"This is the best birthday ever," Fiona said. "And it hasn't even really started yet."

Lindsay perched on a kitchen stool and spun around. "Thanks for being here," she said to everyone in the room. "I promise I won't freak again."

"Tut-tut!" Aunt Mimi said with a few claps of her hands. "We have a feast to consume. Let's eat."

Aunt Mimi brought all of the dishes over to a large, wooden table that was set with giant plates, cups, and a tall vase filled with orange lilies. Madison smiled because, of course, the flowers were her favorite color.

Through one of the windows facing south, the lights of New York City's skyline twinkled under a now-black sky. Clouds crowded in around the tops of buildings. Madison paused briefly to take it all in. Then she scooped a bit of warm macaroni and cheese into her mouth.

After dinner, Aunt Mimi showed everyone in to the back bedrooms. She'd set up two guest rooms with a pair of twin beds in each. The rooms shared a bathroom in the middle, so no one would be very far. Aimee and Fiona decided to bunk together in one room, and Madison and Lindsay took the other room. Aunt Mimi's taste was evident everywhere, from the textured wallpaper to the quilts on the beds to the painted furniture. The girls loved it.

"I wish I had a room like this," Fiona said.

Lindsay threw herself on top of one of the beds. "Aunt Mimi redecorates every three months or so. If you came back in the summer, this whole room would be different."

"Really?" Madison asked.

Lindsay nodded.

"Do you think Aunt Mimi is as rich as Drew's family?" Aimee asked.

"Aim, how can you ask something like that?" Madison cried.

"I don't know," Aimee cracked. "Because I was wondering."

"I think Drew's family is probably a lot richer," Lindsay said. "They have three houses, don't they? Aunt Mimi just has this one apartment. She stays in hotels whenever she goes other places."

Madison's head whirled with all the talk. She wasn't sure if that was from being overwhelmed—or from being overtired.

When she yawned, the other girls yawned, too.

"I can't wait until tomorrow," Fiona said excitedly, stifling another yawn.

"Yes! I want to shop so much more. Aunt Mimi told me she's taking us to this special place for lunch, and we're going to the museum, too," Aimee said.

"I'm glad you're having fun," Lindsay said.

"We are!" Aimee and Fiona said in unison. They headed for their rooms.

Madison followed Lindsay through the shared bathroom into the bedroom where they were planning to sleep.

Lindsay belly-flopped onto her bed.

"Lindsay, what's with you?" Madison asked. "It's your special birthday and ever since you talked to your mom, you've been bummed."

"I don't know," Lindsay said. "I guess I am a little bit sad. Just don't tell the others, okay? I don't want to ruin things."

"Um . . . I think they know that you're upset," Madison said.

"I just don't like getting emotional like that. It's dumb. I don't want to be the party pooper."

"But it's your party!" Madison said.

"Forget about it, Maddie. It's no biggie. I swear. I will be fine."

"What's really the matter, Lindsay?" Madison asked. "Just tell me what's going on. Isn't that what friends are for?"

"You won't understand," Lindsay said.

"Why not?" Madison asked.

"I don't know. Maybe you will." Lindsay's voice dropped to a low, low whisper. "It's not my mom. It's my dad. He was supposed to call me tonight. It's after ten o'clock and he hasn't called. And he won't call now. I know it."

"Why don't you call him?" Madison asked.

"I already did, this morning—twice."

"Oh," Madison said.

"Of course he will call. Eventually."

"Of course he will," Madison said.

The room got very quiet. Off in the distance, they could hear the sound of voices singing high notes. Lindsay said Aunt Mimi always listened to opera late at night.

Lindsay pulled on her pajamas and crawled under the blanket. Madison put on her pj's, too. But instead of getting into bed, she opened her orange bag and yanked out her laptop.

"Would it be okay if I checked my e-mail before we got to sleep?" Madison asked.

"Sure," Lindsay said. "Whatever." She rolled over and pressed her cheek into the soft pillow.

Madison booted up her laptop. She opened her e-mailbox. There were two e-mails. The first was from her dad.

```
From: JeffFinn
To: MadFinn
Subject: Miss You Already
Date: Fri 11 Dec 5:31 PM
```
It's Friday & I miss u already, Honey (and Phin, too). I will miss our regular Sat. dinner tomorrow but I know ur having a blast with the

girls. Have a piece of choc. cake 4
me, ok? Talk 2 u soon.

Love,

Dad

p.s.: What happens when ducks fly
upside down? Send me an e-mail and
tell me!

She smiled at Dad's typically bad riddle. The
answer (of course) was that ducks quack up. As
usual, Dad was telling a riddle he'd already told
before.

Madison skipped to the next name on the list.
Her jaw dropped. Why was public enemy number
one sending Madison an e-mail?

From: Flowr99
To: MadFinn
Subject: Yr science notebk
Date: Fri 11 Dec 6:06 PM
I tried 2 call your house but yr
mom says ur away this weekend. I
think after class today u took
my science notebook. Dunno if
you did it on purpose or by
mistake but either way I need it
back NOW.

Madison burst out laughing.

"What is it?" Lindsay asked groggily. She lifted her head from the pillow and turned toward Madison.

"Ivy Daly," Madison snickered. "She e-mailed me."

Lindsay shot up in bed. Apparently, the one thing that could cure Lindsay of her blahs was good gossip. An e-mail from Ivy qualified.

"Typical," Lindsay said after she read the e-mail aloud.

"I think it's funny," Madison said. "Maybe because I'm here in this incredible place and she's stressing out back home."

"Do you have the notebook?" Lindsay asked.

Madison shook her head. "Not with me. It could be in my locker, but I doubt it. She probably left it in the bathroom or something."

Lindsay and Madison laughed together.

"I bet there's juicy gossip inside that book," Lindsay said.

Madison scratched her head thoughtfully. "I wonder. But I guess even Ivy's allowed to have a secret journal."

Lindsay fell back onto her pillow, eyes open wide. She stared at the ceiling.

"I can't sleep," Lindsay said.

"It's my fault. I woke you up," Madison said. "I'm sorry."

"No, I was awake," Lindsay said. "Look, Maddie, I'm sorry for not talking before. I just don't know what to say—or feel—anymore."

"You mean about your parents?" Madison asked. Lindsay nodded.

"I do understand a little," Madison said. "Don't forget that my parents went through the Big D, too, just last year."

"The Big D?" Lindsay asked. "Oh. Divorce."

"I know it's so rough. Especially when they fight, right?"

"I wish mine *would* fight," Lindsay said. "Instead, they hardly ever speak to each other."

"Really?" Madison said.

"Can I tell you a secret?"

Madison nodded silently. Lindsay took a deep breath.

"My dad moved out a few weeks ago," Lindsay said. She paused. In the half-darkness of the bedroom, her eyes locked on to Madison's. "Please don't tell."

"Tell who?"

"Anyone. Everyone. I don't like to talk about it."

"So is that why your dad hasn't called?" Madison asked.

"Yes," Lindsay let out a tiny gasp and then started to cry. "I think he's angry. My mom kicked him out. She yells all the time."

"Ugh," Madison said. "I know what that's like."

86

"You do?" Lindsay started to cry a little harder.

"I do," Madison said softly.

"He hates me," Lindsay said.

"No, he doesn't," Madison replied.

"He does," Lindsay repeated. She pushed her face down into the pillow to muffle her crying. "I just don't . . . want . . . the others . . . to see me like this . . ."

"Lindsay?" Madison hopped out of bed and went over to her friend.

Lindsay sat up a little.

"Please don't worry," Madison said. "We'll make sure this is your best birthday ever."

"Oh, Maddie, I don't care about my stupid birthday." Lindsay choked back her tears.

Madison gave her a hug and promised never to let go.

Chapter 8

Light streamed in through the curtains in the bedroom where Madison and Lindsay had slept. Madison had awakened at least an hour ago, dragged her laptop into bed, and opened her files.

There was so much to say.

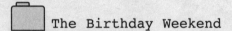 The Birthday Weekend

You could get lost in Aunt Mimi's apartment. I have never been anywhere like this and I have never met anyone like Mimi. Since Ivy has red hair, I had this negative thing about it, but now that I met Mimi, I'd give anything to have red hair. Hers looks like fire. And today she said "we're setting our crazy selves loose on the city!" Part of me wonders if we'll make it back in one piece LOL.

The only problem (and it IS kind of big problem) is Lindsay. Last night she started bumming out. Her parents are in the middle of a Big D and they seem to have forgotten about her. At least that's what it seems like from where I see it. If her dad doesn't call her today I just know she'll be the Big BC, as in Basket Case. I remember one time when my dad was so mad at Mom that he neglected to call ME for a week. I cried myself to sleep with Phinnie every night.

I wish I could make it easier for Lindsay, I really do. But Gramma Helen always told me that the only way to get over something is to go through it. So I just need to be here and to let her know that I'm her friend no matter what.

Rude Awakening: Life has big ships and small ships and all kinds of hardships. But the best ships are friendships. They help you to sail through ANYTHING.

"Maddie!" Aimee whispered very loudly.

Madison jumped and nearly dropped her laptop off the bed. Fiona giggled. Both Aimee and Fiona were still in their pajamas.

"You scared me," Madison said.

"Lindsay's still sleeping," Fiona said. "But it's late, and we have to wake her up."

89

Madison quickly hit SAVE and closed her laptop. She placed it gently on the floor next to the bed. Then she climbed out and linked arms with her other two friends. Slowly, carefully, the three of them climbed atop Lindsay's bed.

Lindsay's mouth was wide open. She wasn't snoring, but she was deep asleep. Her hair was spread out on the pillow like tentacles.

"When I count to three, hold on tight, and start jumping," Aimee whispered.

Madison had to bite her tongue to keep from laughing out loud. Fiona almost lost her balance and fell off the bed. Thankfully she didn't, or she would have dragged everyone with her.

"One . . . two . . . three!"

"WAKE UP! WAKE UP! WAKE UP!"

"Happy Birthday!"

The three BFFs began to jump up and down on the bed. Everything shook. Lindsay rolled over, eyes half open. She pulled a pillow back over her head. But it was hard for her to pretend to sleep anymore. Her bed was in the midst of a devastating earthquake, and she was in danger of flying off onto the floor.

Fiona jumped harder. "Wake up, sleepyhead," she said.

Madison kneeled down and pulled on the pillow. "No more sleeping, birthday girl!" she cried, almost losing her balance.

Lindsay groaned. "Uh . . . uh . . . uh . . . what time is it?"

"Well, it's time for a very big breakfast and a very big day," a voice said from the doorway.

It was, of course, Aunt Mimi standing there. Today she had her red hair pulled up in a giant black hair clip. She wore a shocking-pink top with pencil-thin jeans and leather boots—straight from the pages of the *Fashion Times*. Her lips shimmered pink, too. Up and down her arms she wore gold and silver bangle bracelets that jangled as she moved her arms. Madison loved jewelry like that, jewelry that made music. Her favorite teacher at school, Mrs. Wing, wore similar bracelets.

Lindsay finally popped out from underneath the pillow, nearly knocking everyone else off the bed. She bit her lip and pushed her hair in front of her eyes.

"Am I really thirteen?" Lindsay asked the room.

"Yes! Yes!" Aimee shouted. "Now get up, lazy!"

Madison and Fiona leaned in to tickle Lindsay's side.

Lindsay laughed. "I am not lazy. I'm just . . ."

"Crazy!" Madison shouted.

Aimee, Madison, and Fiona bounced on top of Lindsay and then jumped down off the bed once and for all.

"Well, I'll leave you four to your beauty routines. Meet me in the kitchen in ten, gals," Aunt Mimi said.

Her arms jangled again as she gave a little wave good-bye.

Everyone rushed to the kitchen. It wasn't that the four were particularly hungry. But the sooner the group ate the sooner they got dressed and the sooner they got going.

"Am I considered a real teenager now?" Lindsay asked with a loud groan as she took a bite of granola and fresh yogurt.

"They don't call it thir-*teen* for nothing," Madison said.

"I guess that's a yes," Lindsay said.

"What does turning into a teenager really mean, anyway?" Fiona asked.

"It means now you can drive. You can date. You can vote," Aimee said.

"Aim! I can't do any of those things," Lindsay said, smiling.

"Not *yet*," Aimee said. "But soon. Well, sort of soon."

Everyone laughed.

"Hey, you *can* go shopping!" Madison suggested. "And you can spend the day with your friends walking all over New York City."

"And you can eat whatever you want and go wherever you want," Fiona said.

"And you can get Frrrozen hot chocolate," Aunt Mimi added from where she stood across the room.

"Frrrozen wha'?" Aimee asked.

"Oh, yum," Lindsay said. "You guys haven't lived until you've had one."

"We'll try some on for size at lunch," Aunt Mimi said. "I've got big plans. Let's hustle."

The girls quickly gulped down the rest of their breakfast and raced back to their rooms to get dressed. Aimee and Fiona pulled on jeans with almost the same degree of fadedness, so Aimee decided to change into a ruffled skirt, cable-knit tights, and a very cute pair of Mary Janes. Fiona stayed with the jeans and a scoop-neck sweater. Madison wore a short plaid skirt, nubby stockings, and lace-up black boots. She pulled on her rose-colored sweater coat, along with a green scarf that Gramma Helen had knitted for her a few years back. It was a little stretched out, but she loved the way it matched her woolly hat.

"My goodness, aren't you all the little fashion plates?" Aunt Mimi declared.

"Hardly," Madison quipped. "This jacket is so old."

"Ah, but _trés_ fashionable," Aunt Mimi said with a knowing grin. "Style is what you make it."

Lindsay held her head in her hands. She still hadn't changed out of her pajama bottoms. She stared at her open suitcase with a blank look.

"I'd better stay here," Lindsay said, sounding defeated.

"What are you talking about?" Aimee asked.

"I have nothing to wear," Lindsay shot back.

93

"Why don't you wear your long denim skirt, Lindsay?" Madison suggested. "The one with the leaves embroidered on the front?"

"And the little T-shirt that says, 'Radioactive,'" Fiona added. "I love that T. You have to wear that T."

"Maybe," Lindsay said. But she continued to dawdle, and no one really knew why. After all, it was her birthday—why wasn't she more excited than anyone to hit the sidewalks? Madison guessed that Lindsay had waked up thinking about that phone call from her dad—or rather, the non–phone call. She quietly took Lindsay's hand in hers and squeezed.

"You want to borrow something of mine?" Madison asked. "Not that I have anything very exciting, but . . ."

"You mean it?" Lindsay said.

"My closet is your closet, too, Lindsay," Aunt Mimi reminded her.

Lindsay broke into a wide smile and then disappeared into a side room with both her aunt and Madison. Fiona and Aimee waited in the living room with the big windows. About fifteen minutes later, Lindsay, Madison, and Aunt Mimi walked into the living room.

"Ta-da!" Lindsay said, cocking her hip to one side.

Aimee's eyes bugged out. She could hardly speak (for a change), but Fiona tried.

"You—look—like—amazing—you—look—so— *different*," Fiona stammered.

In the short time it took to vanish into Aunt Mimi's walk-in closet (or walk-in room, depending on how you saw it), Lindsay had transformed herself. She went with the "Radioactive" T-shirt, as Fiona had suggested, and she also wore the long jean skirt. But on top, she wore Aunt Mimi's incredibly cool tweed jacket with ribbon edging and chunky buttons. It made the outfit. Aunt Mimi also lent Lindsay a crocheted sweater that tied over the T with a large blue pom-pom. (Aunt Mimi clearly loved her pom-poms.)

"You have to wear my boots! They will match perfectly!" Fiona declared. "You're a size seven, right?"

Lindsay nodded. "Yes."

Fiona ran into the rooms where they'd slept and came out with a pair of red sheepskin boots with chunky heels. She handed them to Lindsay.

Lindsay pulled on the shoes and stood in front of one of Aunt Mimi's many mirrors.

"I feel better," Lindsay mumbled, turning around to see what she looked like from the back, "so much better."

"You look better, too," Madison said. She grabbed Lindsay's hand again. "I mean, pajamas could be the next trend, but why risk it?"

"It's almost eleven," Aunt Mimi reminded everyone. "Tut-tut."

The weather outside was chilly. Madison wrapped her scarf around her neck twice and braced herself against the wind. The sun was shining brightly and reflected off the glass buildings. And it was that sun that gave Aunt Mimi her first big idea of the day.

"Let's go get some shades," Aunt Mimi said.

So they raced across three city blocks toward an entrance to Central Park near Fifty-ninth Street where, just outside the park on the corner, two guys stood behind a table that was covered with sunglasses.

"Take your pick," Aunt Mimi said to everyone, gesturing at the table.

"You're joking," Aimee said.

"We need to get our cool on," Aunt Mimi said.

Fiona laughed out loud. She reached for a pair of reddish tortoiseshell frames with gray lenses. They looked perfect with her hair, which was braided and adorned with amber and red beads.

"I love those," Madison said.

"Me, too," Lindsay said. She scanned the table looking for a pair of her own.

"Try these, Lindsay," Madison said, handing her a pair of sleek silver (or fake silver) frames. Then she grabbed thick orange frames for herself.

Lindsay balanced the glasses on the bridge of her nose and posed.

"Are they me?"

"Abso-tootly!" Aunt Mimi said. She held her hands up. "Where's the camera?"

"I'm thinking pink," Aimee announced as she showed off the pair she liked the best. Teeny rhinestones were embedded on the edges of the frame.

"Another hit!" Aunt Mimi declared as she paid the vendor for all four pairs of glasses.

They continued back down the street and boarded a bus to cross town. It was only a short while before they arrived in front of Bloomingdale's department store. Aunt Mimi suggested that they use the Lexington Avenue entrance and travel through the store (past walls and walls of mirrors), to the exit on Third Avenue. It was a shortcut to the place where they'd be having lunch.

Madison, Fiona, Aimee, and Lindsay could hardly catch their breath inside Bloomingdale's; there was so much to see and so much to buy. Madison recalled what she had told Mom when she first got permission to come on the weekend trip. She'd promised not to spend a lot of money shopping. But this store made her want to change all of that. She wanted to shop, shop, shop—yes, until she dropped.

Aimee was infatuated with the mirrors that seemed to be everywhere on the walls of the store's interior. She could hardly walk a few steps without turning to look at her reflection or without pausing to try a new dance step.

"Show-off," Madison joked as they walked along.

Lindsay chuckled.

"Hold on!" Aunt Mimi held her hands out as though she were stopping traffic. "Brainstorm. I just got another idea."

She dragged all four girls over to a long counter in the beauty department. A large, older woman wearing a white smock greeted Aunt Mimi with a kiss on both cheeks.

"We were just in the neighborhood, Hilde. And we've got a few gals here who need to look pretty as a picture today," Aunt Mimi said, rubbing her gloved hands together. "Can you help?"

"Hello, girls!" the woman said. She coughed and eyeballed them. "Oh, these are all such pretty ones, Mimi."

The woman's accent sounded Russian, Madison thought, although she really didn't know the difference between one foreign accent and the next. Aunt Mimi bragged that Hilde was the best makeup artist in all of New York City. Madison wasn't sure that was true, but it didn't matter. What mattered was that today someone—anyone—was going to make Madison, Aimee, Fiona, *and* Lindsay up.

The four friends squealed with delight.

Aimee hopped up into the makeover chair first. Hilde pulled Aimee's blond hair back using some hair clips and applied a light dusting of powder, some pale pink shadow, and lipstick. After Aimee was done, Fiona sat in the chair, and then Lindsay, and finally Madison. Hilde gave Madison extra-special treatment, pulling her hair into some kind of cool twist—a cross between a French braid and a slip-knot.

Aunt Mimi waved her arms around like a proud peacock once Hilde had finished, cooing at the girls. After that, they all moved through the rest of Bloomingdale's feeling like cover girls. Now the four were stopping to glance at their reflections on the walls; even Lindsay, who normally detested mirrors, looked.

"We look good, don't we?" Madison asked.

"Yeah," Aimee said. "Too bad Ivy isn't here so we could show her and her dumb drones up."

"This is the best day ever," Fiona gushed. She moved her head back and forth, and the beads on her braids clinked.

"This is definitely the best birthday I ever had," Lindsay said. "And I was going to stay home in my pajamas? Thanks for rescuing me."

Madison took Lindsay's arm and swung it in time with her own.

"Here we go!" Aunt Mimi cried as the row of glass doors appeared before them. They'd reached the opposite side of the store, on Third Avenue. Now it was only a few blocks more, Aunt Mimi said, until they had lunch.

Serendipity, the restaurant with the Frrrozen hot chocolate, had a line out the door into the street. People had their scarves and coats pulled around them tightly to protect them from the wind. The East River was only a block or so away, and the gusts of air off the water could get very cold at times.

Although the line seemed long at first, it really wasn't—at least not with Aunt Mimi leading the way. She waltzed right up to the hostess, who promptly led the girls and Aunt Mimi to one of the best tables in the place. There, they were presented with the hugest menus Madison had ever seen.

They noshed on sandwiches, sweet-potato fries, and fruit salad before getting to the main course, or at least the main reason they were there. Aunt Mimi ordered.

"Decaf for me and two Frrrozen hot chocolates for the troops," she told the waiter.

When the drinks arrived, in widemouthed glasses teeming with thick whipped cream and chocolate shavings, Madison thought she would pass out. They needed to pair up and share. Aimee and Fiona quickly scooped out a taste from one glass. Then Lindsay handed Madison a straw.

"Shall we?" Lindsay said smiling, armed with a long straw of her own.

Aunt Mimi pulled her small digital camera from her bag and asked the girls to pose.

"Smile, friends!" Aunt Mimi said.

Madison couldn't believe that a single day could be so perfect. She'd nearly forgotten everything about her boring existence back in Far Hills.

Well, almost.

In the back of her mind, as she sat there with icy lips sharing the cold, delicious drink with Lindsay, Madison wondered what it would be like to sip one of Serendipity's Frrrozen hot chocolates with a certain someone else—a certain someone named Hart Jones.

What would a Frrrozen hot chocolate kiss taste like?

Chapter 9

After elbowing their way back through the line outside Serendipity, Aunt Mimi and the girls walked uptown about ten blocks. Then they headed west toward Central Park.

"Where to now?" Lindsay asked. She seemed to have forgotten all about her dad and the question of whether he would call her. Her whole mood had lifted, even though her feet were a little tired.

"Well, I thought we'd make a trip across the park to the American Museum of Natural History. The planetarium has a new show. But first, first, we have a special stop for Madison," Aunt Mimi said. She rubbed her hands together and grinned.

Madison smiled. "A special stop for *me*?"

Aunt Mimi nodded.

"No secrets! What is it?" Fiona asked excitedly. "Is it some cool laptop computer store?"

Aunt Mimi shook her head.

"A pet store with pugs like Phinnie?" Lindsay guessed.

"Nope," Aunt Mimi said. "Let's go-go!"

Everyone hustled along the sidewalk for several more blocks, following neatly behind Aunt Mimi until she stopped at a certain corner.

"Ah, we've arrived," Aunt Mimi said, extending her hands.

They stood there as the traffic whizzed past. A bus beeped its horn, and a couple of pigeons flapped above their heads from their perch on a storefront ledge.

Madison shrugged. "Um . . . Aunt Mimi, I'm sorry, but I don't get it."

Aunt Mimi smiled. "Look around."

"Oh!" Aimee started to laugh. "I get it!" she yelled. Aimee pointed up to the street sign.

"Madison Avenue!" Lindsay said aloud. She grabbed Madison in a huge hug. "Aunt Mimi, you have to take a picture right now."

"Pictures!" Aunt Mimi gasped. "That sounds like a perfectly yummy idea." She retrieved her digital camera and pointed it at the girls. "Closer; get closer. . . ." she said.

"Aunt Mimi, we couldn't be any closer!" Lindsay cried.

Everyone laughed out loud.

The smell of pretzels wafted in the air and Madison breathed deeply. She remembered when her parents had taken her to the city to see the Big Apple Circus for the first time. They'd driven down Madison Avenue and pointed out all of the colorful shops before turning in to the park. It seemed like only yesterday, but it was already half of her life ago.

"Aunt Mimi, are we going shopping again?" Lindsay asked, sounding slightly disappointed. "It's not that I don't want to shop, but it's almost two-something and we should probably go to the museum if we're going to go, right? I mean . . . I don't know what everyone else would like to see, but I would like to see the light show. I mean . . . if no one else minds. . . ."

"Mind? Of course we don't mind!" Fiona declared.

"Of course," Madison agreed.

"Hey, it's *your* birthday," Aimee said. "Your rules."

"Indeedy," Aunt Mimi said with a deferential bow of her head. "As the birthday girl wishes. Let's hoof it to the park entrance. We can take a bus across and get to the planetarium—pronto."

The bus only took ten minutes, and then they were standing in front of the all-glass Rose Planetarium on the corner of Eighty-first Street and

Central Park West. Already the day had turned into a citywide exploration—and Lindsay was loving every minute. She grabbed Madison's wrist and pulled her up the steps to the door of the planetarium.

Madison laughed to herself. She knew this was more the kind of place her BFF liked. Lindsay was game for fashion makeovers, but what mattered a lot more to her was the chance to learn something new. She was always sort of studying. Of course, it wasn't studying for the test coming up on Monday, but it was the next best thing.

Lindsay's eyes opened wide when they stepped into the planetarium. Above their heads Madison saw the suspended sculptures of planets and moons hovering from barely visible wires.

"This is . . . awesome," Fiona said as she walked inside.

Chatterbox Aimee was speechless. No opinions, just stares. She looked up at the enormous sphere overhead that was supposed to be the sun. Her jaw dropped.

Aunt Mimi shuffled off to the ticket booth and got their tickets for a new exhibit called "Are We Alone in the Galaxy?" They lucked out and didn't have to wait in a very long line to get inside. After only half an hour they were sitting in a row in the semidarkness along with hundreds of other kids, parents, and tourists speaking languages like French, Japanese, and Farsi.

The ceiling of the planetarium theater was shaped like a bubble, a dark, curved, painted sky with bumps and shapes. It reminded Madison of the main room at Grand Central Station. Everywhere they had gone in New York so far, the sky and stars had watched over them, taking good care of Madison and friends.

The seats in the auditorium reclined so that visitors could lean back and survey the sky from a nearly prone position. After all the makeovers, the hot chocolate, and the walking around the city, Madison and her friends were relieved to lie down.

"I think I could fall asleep right here," Fiona said with a little yawn.

"No, you won't," Aimee said softly. She motioned down a few rows. "Not with those cute boys ahead of us," she said.

Fiona sat back up. "Huh? Who?"

"They're not *that* cute," Madison said.

Lindsay didn't make any comment. She pushed her chair back and closed her eyes. After a moment, Madison tapped Lindsay's shoulder.

"Are you okay?" Madison asked.

Lindsay blinked. Madison could see that her eyes were wet.

"Are you *crying*?" Madison whispered. No one else could hear. Aimee and Fiona were too busy talking about the boys, who had now noticed them, too.

Lindsay didn't care about any of that. "I'm not

crying," she sniffled to Madison. "Well, I am, but just a little. I was just thinking of Dad."

"What about him?" Madison asked.

"He never takes me places like this," she said.

"Lindsay," Madison whispered. "You have to stop worrying."

Lindsay frowned. "Sometimes my dad makes me feel like *I'm* the jerk."

Madison raised an eyebrow. "But you're not," she said. "Remember?"

All at once, a voice boomed through the loud-speaker: *Please refrain from taking photographs during the show. There are safety lights in the aisles if you need to exit the auditorium. . . .*

As the announcements continued, the lights went off, except for one teeny-tiny spotlight in a corner of the ceiling.

Aimee giggled, which made Fiona giggle. Madison was sure Aunt Mimi would lean over and say, "Shhh!" Instead, she giggled, too. They weren't the only ones. An entire school group had a case of the giggles on the other side of the room.

Then a different recorded voice began to speak. The sound echoed in the cold room. Why was it so cold all of a sudden? Madison wondered. Except for the whispering and laughter all around them, it felt as if they could be lying on a blanket out in the middle of some real field watching a real sky. Maybe the cold was all in her head, Madison thought.

107

The ceiling became a video-projection screen with images of the sky quickly turning to pictures of dark, deep water, as if the people in the audience were diving into the sea. The narrator described life way down in the furthest depths of the ocean. Even in that cold darkness, where the water pressure was so intense, creatures lived. The screen showed tube worms, clams, and microbes.

Lindsay wasn't crying anymore. She was listening intently. Madison was happy to see her friend cheered up by what she heard.

After a few more moments underwater, the screen shifted again to the skies. It showed space, stars, and planets.

At one point, the giant projector showed the glowing image of a large moon. It was Europa, one of the moons of Jupiter. Madison leaned back as far as she could in the chair. She tried to imagine what it would be like to fly into space, to soar above the earth in a rocket, to venture to the edges of the universe.

Sometimes, she thought, life felt that foreign to her. It seemed as if she were always investigating or exploring or at least just trying to figure stuff out. And just when she believed that she'd finally (finally!) reached some new frontier, like getting a real date with Hart, something strange would happen to throw her off course. Was *that* the way the universe was supposed to work?

The stars flashed overhead while music played soft and low. Out of the corner of one eye Madison spotted Lindsay with her own eyes fixed on the ceiling. She was feeling better, fortunately. Her moments of being upset never seemed to last long. They were just coming more frequently now, since she'd confided in everyone about her father.

"You should make a wish," Madison whispered.

"Huh?"

"There are a million stars glittering up there," Madison said. "Make a wish on one of them."

"You're right," Lindsay said.

Madison made her own wish. She wished that Lindsay would have a good birthday—and that her dad would show up. She figured that if she made the same exact wish that she knew her friend was making it would have twice as much chance of coming true.

When the lights came back up again, Aimee and Fiona were still stifling a few giggles. Aimee pointed to the boys a few rows up, the same ones they had been checking out before the show.

"Let's follow them," she suggested as a goof. But Aunt Mimi heard her and cleared her throat. "Ahem . . . we will do no following, ladies," she said. It was the very first time Madison had seen—and heard— the grown-up in Lindsay's aunt. Aunt Mimi now sounded a little more like Mom and the other mothers and less like the cool, eccentric relative one liked to show off to friends.

109

Aimee and Fiona, however, were not deterred.

"We'll probably see those boys outside, anyway," Fiona said. "We're taking a walk on the Cosmic Pathway."

Aunt Mimi rolled her eyes. "Let's go, my darlings."

"Aunt Mimi," Lindsay said as they stood up and shimmied out of their row and into the main aisle. "Can you check your cell phone? Did Dad call you while we were in here?"

Aunt Mimi clicked her phone on, but there were no messages.

A deflated Lindsay walked off by herself. Madison hurried after her, followed by Aimee and Fiona.

As it happened, the boys from the auditorium were headed in the same direction. Aimee collided with one of them near a water fountain.

"Sorry," said the boy, who had tousled blond hair. "I didn't see you."

"Yeah, right," Lindsay whispered to Madison.

Madison laughed, and all the boys turned to look.

Fiona made a face that seemed to say, "Maddie, how could you be so embarrassing!" Madison wanted to say, "How can you be looking at some other cute guy when you supposedly like Egg, the cute guy who is one of my friends?" Of course Madison knew the answer. It didn't matter how

110

much you liked someone. If there was a really cute, or Cute (with a capital C) guy in the room, checking him out was a necessity.

Another one of the cute guys (there were three in all), sidled up to Lindsay. Madison realized that these boys were older—by at least two or maybe even three years. Aunt Mimi stood by and let the girls talk, but she had her eye on everyone the entire time.

"You guys live in New York?" a brown-haired guy with glasses asked Aimee.

Lindsay leaned into Madison again. "He looks like Hart," she said quietly.

Madison looked him over. In her opinion, he looked nothing like her crush. But this guy was cute—little-c cute, but cute nonetheless.

"We live in New York," Fiona answered at last. She looked over at Aunt Mimi to see if her answer was okay.

These boys were full of questions.

"Go to school in the city?" another one asked.

"Nope." It was Aimee who answered this time.

"Are you two sisters?" a boy with really short hair, almost a crew cut, asked Madison, referring to her and Lindsay.

"Sisters?" Lindsay said. She cracked a smile.

"Practically," Madison replied.

"You look alike," the boy said. "Hey, you want to hang out down by the . . ."

Aunt Mimi took that as her cue to step in.

"Sorry, boys, we've got a tight schedule today. No can do," she said abruptly, almost shooing the boys away.

They turned away, grumbling. "See you later," the blond one said.

Aunt Mimi stood there with her hands on her hips until they had almost disappeared from view.

"Smart alecks," she said. Then she laughed. "But they are cute."

Lindsay shrugged. "Boys can be so annoying," she said. "But I liked the part about us being sisters, Maddie."

"You do look a little bit alike," Fiona said. "I always thought that, but I never actually said it."

"Yeah," Aimee agreed. "You have practically the same hair."

"And the same style," Fiona said.

"And the same heart," Aunt Mimi added.

"Hart? Oh, no!" Madison cried, pretending to be emotional at the mention of his name.

The group burst into laughter at Madison's antics. Slowly, they walked farther along the Cosmic Pathway toward the gift shop. It was getting late. They needed to purchase souvenirs, then hit the pavement once again, and then to go back to Aunt Mimi's and get dressed for the big birthday dinner.

"Yo! See you later!" a voice called from out of nowhere.

It was actually coming from below.

Madison and the others peered over the walkway wall. One level below, on the curve of another ramp, stood the three boys who had been asking them questions.

"Check that out," said Lindsay.

"Yeah," Aimee joked. "So I guess we really aren't alone in the galaxy."

Chapter 10

 Our Never-Ending Day

Rude Awakening: If this is the city that never sleeps, then why am I so tired? I never imagined life in New York could be this much fun. I also never knew power-shopping could be this much work.

It is now exactly 5:20. Wow I am wiped.

I just loved walking down the street with Aunt Mimi. She knows ALL about ALL the buildings in NY. She was like a tour guide the way she could point to any old skyscraper or apartment or embassy and tell us when it was built and what style architecture it was. It's not like I understood about architecture or anything, but I loved hearing her talk. I always thought I was a real New Yorker, but I don't know that stuff. Aunt Mimi is the real New Yorker.

The Natural History museum is huge. I wished we could have seen the dinosaurs inside the main part of the museum, but the Rose Center for Earth and Space was enough for today. We walked and walked on this one ramp called the Cosmic Pathway trying to get away from these cute guys who kept following us. We ducked into the Big Dipper Café and then finally ditched them at the gift shop where (it must be noted) I bought myself a cool foil sticker of Mars for my flute case. I also got two super-bouncy balls: one that looks like the moon and another one that looks like Earth.

The walking display was the COOLEST. Just one step covered something like 75 million years of evolution. I couldn't believe that humans were only one teeny, teeny mark at the end of the timeline. We're like nothing compared to the time before we existed. I need to pay more attention in Mr. Danehy's science class when he starts talking about the planets and space, right? Right!!!

"Maddie, are you still writing? We have to hurry," Fiona said. She was changing into a smock dress and turtleneck and trying hard not to smudge what was left of her makeup from the Bloomingdale's makeover. Everyone was getting ready to go out for the big birthday dinner, and Madison still needed to fix her hair and get ready, too.

"I know, I know, I'm done," Madison answered. She clicked the laptop shut and slid it underneath the bed where she'd slept the night before.

Lindsay came out of the bathroom wearing a turtleneck sweater and wraparound top that was made from kimono fabric. She had paired it with a long denim skirt. Mrs. Frost, Lindsay's mother, followed behind her daughter, brushing nonexistent lint off Lindsay's back.

Mrs. Frost had arrived at the apartment that afternoon while the girls had been out shopping. She appeared just as decked out as her sister, Mimi, with fancy shoes and jewelry on, only Mrs. Frost's style was way more conservative than her sister's style. But although Aunt Mimi and Mrs. Frost were opposites in many ways, when they were together they talked the same and had the same mannerisms.

According to Lindsay, the sisters hadn't always been so close. During college, they hardly ever spoke to each other. But lately they had been spending a lot more time together. Lindsay was part of the reason. Aunt Mimi loved to spoil her niece. But another reason was the pending divorce. When times were tough, friends rallied, but sisters survived—together.

"Doesn't my daughter look like the queen of the birthday ball?" Mrs. Frost asked aloud. "Lindsay, darling, you are exquisite. Let's put a flower in your hair."

"Oh, Mom," Lindsay groaned.

"You have to start dressing like this at home," Aimee said. "Every guy in our class will fall in like with you."

Madison laughed. "What's so great about that?"

"What isn't great about it?" Fiona said.

"I have one word for you," Madison said. "Lance." She laughed out loud. Lance was a dorky seventh grader whom they always made fun of.

"Okay, I get your point," Fiona said, smiling.

"It is now six. Our reservation is for seven," Aunt Mimi reminded everyone.

"Yikes," Madison blurted. "I better get my clothes on—fast."

"Yeah, Maddie, I don't want to be late to the restaurant," Lindsay said.

"Okeydokey, karaoke," Madison said, bouncing on tiptoe into the bathroom. It wouldn't take her more than five minutes to put on a new skirt and top, even if they were a little wrinkled from being crammed into Madison's suitcase.

Aimee and Fiona sat on one of the many sofas while Madison and Lindsay finished dressing. Mrs. Frost dashed into the bathroom herself to put on more blusher and eyeliner.

117

Lindsay paced the floor outside the bathroom door. "Mom? You know that Dad never called me, right? Are you sure he'll be there?" she asked. "He promised he'd be there, but do you really think he'll show up?"

Mrs. Frost opened the bathroom door and poked her head out.

"You know your father has a lot going on these days," Mrs. Frost said to Lindsay. "He told me the last time we spoke that he would *try* to make it."

"I really want him to be there," Lindsay said. "I want him to sing Happy Birthday. I want him to see my makeover."

Mrs. Frost smiled. "Oh, you do look lovely, sweetheart," she said. "Your father would be very impressed."

Lindsay embraced her mom. Her tears had been close to the surface since the previous day. Madison wondered if Lindsay would start crying again as she had in the planetarium.

But Lindsay didn't. She smoothed out the wrinkles in her kimono-cloth top and slipped on an oversize blue wool poncho—another loan from her aunt.

"I'm ready," Lindsay said.

Aimee and Fiona pulled on their jackets, too.

"Sorry for being such a slowpoke," Madison said.

The six party girls (including Mrs. Frost and Aunt Mimi) made their way out to the hall and into the private elevator to the lobby. Aunt Mimi had ordered two cabs; the doorman had the cars waiting by the curb.

"I know we've said it a hundred times already this weekend, but this is the most exciting birthday *ever*," Madison whispered to Lindsay when they were squished together in the back of one of the taxis.

Lindsay smiled. "I know," she said. "But that's thanks to you guys. I don't know what I would do if you weren't here. It wouldn't be the same, would it?"

They drove up Park Avenue toward the restaurant, which was located on the Upper East Side. It seemed as if they had to stop for another traffic light every two blocks or so, but Madison didn't mind the slower ride. It gave her and Lindsay a chance to talk some more.

"I was thinking about what you said last night," Lindsay said. "About the Big D and how hard it was for you. But I think things will be different for me. I really do. What if my parents decide they don't even *want* to split up?"

"Haven't they already decided?"

Lindsay shrugged. "Yeah. But things can change. People can change. Can't they?"

"Sometimes," Madison said.

Of course, what Madison wanted to say was

119

"Beware, they can change; sure they can—for the *worse*." Madison's mom and dad had never been yellers; but after the Big D, everything had been expressed with a scream. Before the divorce, they would make big dinners together and listen to classical music while they cooked. After the divorce, there was no time for that. Mom plunged into a more hectic work schedule. Dad moved away. The Big D ushered in the era of takeout and no talking. Life got twice as busy. Madison was never sure why.

"I know I'm supposed to be super happy because it's my birthday. But I only wish that . . . oh, forget it, I already made that wish at the planetarium."

"Your dad?" Madison asked.

Lindsay stared out the window. "Did you ever wish . . . ?" Her voice trailed off.

Madison sighed. She leaned into her friend. "Yes," she said.

The sign outside the restaurant read DELICIOUS in bold neon letters. Inside were round metal tables surrounded by soft, red-cushioned chairs. Each table had been decorated with a vase of wheat, not flowers. The waiters wore red smocks. The tables were packed, which meant that the volume inside the restaurant was louder than loud.

Aunt Mimi pulled her usual strings and got them seated quickly. Madison breathed a sigh of relief when she noticed that the table was set for seven.

That meant there was still a place setting for Mr. Frost. She had her fingers and toes crossed that he would show up.

He *had* to show up.

But Madison also believed in omens, and a bad one happened the moment they sat down. Fiona knocked over Mrs. Frost's glass of merlot.

"Oh, *no*!" Fiona shrieked when she saw Aunt Mimi's long, cream-colored scarf. It now had a red splatter on it.

Two waiters rushed over.

Aunt Mimi gave Fiona a wink. "I think I look good in wine stain," she joked, removing her scarf. She folded it neatly on the table and asked the waiter for some club soda.

Aimee leaned into Fiona. "Good one," she said.

"I didn't mean it . . ." Fiona moaned. She looked as though she were about to burst into serious sobs. Next to her, Lindsay was looking sadder than sad, too.

"Such long faces for a party?" Mrs. Frost commented. "Girls, let's have a good time. Come on. Let's order something fun."

Aunt Mimi, Aimee, Fiona, and Mrs. Frost scanned their menus.

Madison was busy eyeing Lindsay. She could tell that her friend's sad expression meant that her mind was elsewhere. Lindsay kept glancing over at the door.

"What time is it?" Lindsay asked aloud.

Aunt Mimi glanced at her dark green, oversize

watch face. "Seven-fifteen," Aunt Mimi said. "Why don't you pick out something to nibble?" she advised her niece.

"Yes, Lindsay, this is your party, dear," Mrs. Frost said. Then she added in a soft voice, "Please stop pouting."

Madison squirmed a little in her chair. She could tell that Aimee and Fiona were uncomfortable, too. Mrs. Frost and Aunt Mimi exchanged furtive glances. The clock ticked. The waiter took their lengthy orders, but their table remained mostly silent. He brought fresh bread, and everyone dug in to the basket. The best way to fight uncertainty seemed obvious: eat.

By the time it was seven-forty-five, however, only one thing seemed certain. There was no sign of Mr. Frost's arriving. He hadn't called. He hadn't left a message on Aunt Mimi's or Mrs. Frost's phone.

"Ever hear the one about the birthday cat?" Madison asked.

Mrs. Frost raised her eyebrows. "No, I have not," she said.

"Tell us, Maddie!" Aunt Mimi encouraged Madison.

"Well," Madison began, remembering a bad joke that her dad had shared with her once. But then, in the middle of speaking, she drew a blank. Her expression slackened. "I . . . I . . . forgot," Madison admitted.

"Forgot?" Mrs. Frost asked, looking confused.

Aimee and Fiona cracked up. Even Aunt Mimi seemed to find Madison's forgetfulness amusing. But Lindsay just sat there, poking a finger into her mouth, gnawing on the newly manicured, gorgeous, makeover nails. She wasn't used to the polish, and Madison could tell she was worlds away.

How embarrassing, Madison thought. This is a disaster.

At least dinner was on its way. After the waiter brought their food, the group ate their peppered swordfish and basil chicken and vegetarian risotto—and did a lot more chewing than talking. Waiters also brought side dishes of baby corn; sliced tomatoes sprinkled with cilantro, and roasted Jerusalem artichokes, which Madison thought tasted more like little potatoes than anything else. The friends poked forks into one another's food, tasting as much as they possibly could. Although Aimee and Madison both had their moments of being picky eaters, they tried all the food on the table. Lindsay was the only one of them who didn't eat very much. She tasted some chicken and put her fork back down.

"Everything really is so . . . well . . . what's the word I'm looking for?" Mrs. Frost said, attempting to make a little play on words on the name of the establishment. "Delicious?"

"Ha-ha," Aimee and Fiona giggled politely. "Sure thing," they said in unison.

123

As they finished the meal, an old cuckoo clock chimed exactly nine times.

"Nine? It's already nine?" Lindsay said. "I really thought he might come."

"Look, Lindsay, don't give up. He may still show up," Mrs. Frost said, trying to make even more excuses for her estranged husband. "I have my cell phone here, so let me check again. Maybe he just got stuck in traffic."

Lindsay looked forlorn.

"Stuck in traffic for almost two hours?" Lindsay asked.

No one said anything.

Then Aunt Mimi cleared her throat. "Enough of this talk," she said assertively. "I think what this group of gals needs is an extra-extra-large dose of dark chocolate. What do you say, Lindsay? It's your favorite."

Uncharacteristically, a deflated Lindsay shook her head.

"No, thanks," she said.

"No?" Aunt Mimi gasped. "Hmph! We'll see about that." She crooked a finger and signaled to the server. From across the restaurant he nodded. Then he disappeared into the back.

Fiona and Aimee tried to kick Madison under the table, but they booted Mrs. Frost by mistake instead.

"Ouch!" Mrs. Frost exclaimed. Then she broke into a smile. "Was that your foot, Lindsay?"

"Yeah, who's playing soccer under the table?" Aimee asked. "Fiona?"

"Very funny, Aim," Fiona said.

Everyone laughed. But Lindsay didn't even bat an eyelash. She was still spacing out when the waiter—or when *five* waiters emerged from the kitchen carrying a large, brown, frosted cake covered with sparklers.

"Happy bertday to eww, happy bertday to eww." The waiters sang in a funny accent. Aunt Mimi leaned over to Madison. "This place is famous for its birthday surprises," she whispered. "Isn't this just de-lish?"

Aimee and Fiona had their eyes locked on the waiters and the cake, but Madison was looking at Lindsay. Her friend still looked so sad. She wasn't even watching the cake or the waiters. She was still staring at the front door of the restaurant.

She was still waiting for Mr. Frost to appear.

Aunt Mimi decided to get the cake wrapped to go. She said they could eat it for breakfast. Fiona loved that idea.

"Please don't be sad," Madison said to Lindsay. "Everything will work out. It always does. Gramma Helen tells me that, and she's usually right about stuff."

"Well, she never met my dad," Lindsay grumbled.

Mrs. Frost made an uncomfortable face. "Lindsay, I think you need to stop this. I know it's your birthday, and I know you're disappointed, but your father . . ."

Aunt Mimi stood up, and Madison knew exactly why; she wanted to change the subject. Aimee and Fiona knew it, too. Madison shot them both a glance. They had to do something to cheer Lindsay up.

The waiters brought the check. Aunt Mimi paid, and they all retrieved their coats from the checkroom at the front of the restaurant. Lindsay wasn't saying much.

Aunt Mimi put an arm around Lindsay's shoulder and grabbed Madison with the other arm.

"Girls, I never noticed before this very minute," she whispered, "but you two look like sisters. Same hair, same beautiful smile."

"Aunt Mimi, come on," Lindsay said. She started to pull away, but then she stopped herself and broke into a huge smile. "Sisters?"

"We've heard that before," Madison said.

"Sometimes it does feel like we're all related, don't you think?" Fiona added. "I mean, none of us has any real sisters."

In that moment, something shifted. Lindsay seemed happier, almost as if she'd forgotten about the trouble with her dad for a flickering moment.

The door to the restaurant blew open next to them as a large crowd of people pushed their way in. The air outside was nippy. The four friends huddled together against the cold.

"Shall we?" Aunt Mimi said, indicating the exit. "We have presents to open back at my place."

"Yes, let's go," Mrs. Frost said. "Let's make the rest of your birthday great, Lindsay."

"Greater than great," Madison said, taking Lindsay's arm in hers as they pushed their way through the door.

Chapter 11

"Good evening, ladies," George said as they walked into the lobby of Aunt Mimi's building. "How was the big birthday?"

"Just dreamy, George," replied Mrs. Frost.

"Yes, Delicious was a success. Thanks for the recommendation," Aunt Mimi added.

George nodded. "Glad to help."

They rode the elevator upstairs, trying hard not to fall asleep standing up. It had been a long day and an even longer night. Everyone had aching feet from walking around so much, except Aunt Mimi, who prided herself on her ability to march all over New York City in high-heeled boots and shoes without getting blisters. Madison knew she couldn't walk a single block in heels. She'd tried on a pair of Mom's shoes once and nearly toppled down the stairs.

Stepping into Aunt Mimi's apartment felt like being wrapped in a blanket. Aunt Mimi immediately went over to the enormous fireplace in the living room and lit the logs that were sitting there. The fire started with a slow crackle, and soon the scent of woodsmoke was in the air. Madison and her friends collapsed onto the couches just as they had the day before.

"I want you to open your gifts," Aimee said.

Lindsay's eyes lit up. "Oh, yeah," she said with a sly smile. "I guess that will cheer me up, won't it?"

Mrs. Frost put on the teakettle and turned the stereo on low. Madison marveled at how civilized everything felt there, not like the birthday parties she was used to back in Far Hills, with loud music and screaming and stuff strewn everywhere. A part of her missed the chaos, but another part of her loved this. There was something calm and safe about being in this apartment, this cocoon, tucked away from the December cold.

Everyone ran to their bedrooms to retrieve their presents for Lindsay. They met back in front of the fireplace. Aunt Mimi had placed huge pillows on the floor for everyone to sit on.

"Open mine first!" Fiona said with a wide grin. She handed Lindsay a large, rectangular package.

Lindsay smiled and shook it. "No loose parts," she

joked. She ripped the paper open to reveal a copy of *Dragons and Fairies, Oh, My!* The binding was red leather with gold lettering.

"It's beautiful," Lindsay said.

"I know you said something the other day about liking fantasy, and I know how much you like to read, and my mom saw this when we were at Aimee's dad's bookstore, actually . . ." Fiona babbled. "It looked so cool."

Lindsay thanked Fiona. Then she reached for another, larger gift that was perched on the edge of the sofa.

"That's a little something from me," Aunt Mimi said.

"Aunt Mimi, you already gave me this party," Lindsay said.

"Oh, pish posh," Aunt Mimi cried. "Just open it, already."

Inside a purple satin box Lindsay found a leather backpack with patches of tapestry sewn together on it and a beautiful silver buckle at the center.

"That is awesome!" Aimee cried.

"It's like a college backpack," Madison said.

Lindsay slung it over one shoulder and modeled it for the room.

"You can use it for school," Aunt Mimi suggested. "It's even big enough for a laptop computer."

"When I get one . . ." Lindsay said.

Madison smiled. She knew how much Lindsay

wanted to have the same kind of computer she had.

Lindsay reached way over to give Aunt Mimi a smooch and nearly fell on top of another gift.

"Careful!" Aimee cautioned her. "Don't crush my present."

Lindsay leaned back and tore the tape off the top of Aimee's gift. It was a square box. No one seemed to have any idea what was in it.

Neither did Lindsay. She opened the box and fluffed out the tissue paper inside. But she found nothing.

"Um . . . Aimee . . . I don't mean to be rude, but . . . " Lindsay stammered.

"Look at the bottom," Aimee said.

Lindsay looked underneath all of the paper. There, taped to the bottom of the box, was a gift card. It was a card to be used at Aimee's dad's bookstore.

"Oh, wow!" Lindsay cried. "I can buy more books."

Madison wrinkled her nose. "Aim, why did you wrap it in that big box?"

"Because!" Aimee said. "Everyone always gives those gift cards in a plain wrapper or envelope, and I'm sorry, but that is just *not* as much fun as opening up a box with tissue paper."

The girls laughed.

Mrs. Frost stepped into the center of the room with a large envelope. She placed it on the sofa.

"Something from your mother," she said. "For you, for us."

Lindsay tore open the top of the envelope. Out slid two tickets.

"Theater tickets!" Lindsay exclaimed. "I told you that was what I wanted. These are amazing, Mom."

"Read the note," Mrs. Frost insisted.

Lindsay read it aloud.

> *For my darling daughter*
> *Look to the moon for all your dreams.*
> *The stars hold all the secrets.*
> *No matter what happens, I am always*
> *   here for you.*
>
> *   Love, Mom*
> *P.S.: Any show you want, any dinner you*
> *   want, anything you want!*

"Did you know we were going to the planetarium today?" Aimee asked.

Mrs. Frost shook her head. "I'm afraid not. That's just one of those coincidences, I guess. I've got stars on the brain."

"I don't believe in coincidences," Aunt Mimi said matter-of-factly. "I believe in destiny."

Madison liked the sound of that. "Um . . . here's my present," she said sheepishly as she passed a small gift box to Lindsay. "I was going to get you this picture frame, but then I saw this, and I liked it way better."

Lindsay gave Madison a funny look and then

opened the little box, lifting the lid to find a charm suspended on a silver chain.

Lindsay reached into the box and pulled out the necklace. The charm was shaped like a book.

"So cool," Fiona gushed. "I want one."

"Me, too!" Aimee said. "We should get them for all four of us."

"That's a grand idea," Aunt Mimi said.

Mrs. Frost was smiling, too. "Lindsay, you certainly are lucky to have such a special crew of friends. My goodness."

Ding-a-ling-a-ling.

"What was that?" Madison asked.

"Oh," Lindsay said. "Aunt Mimi's intercom."

"I wonder what George wants," Aunt Mimi said as she strode across the living room to get to the intercom receiver located in the outer hallway.

The girls helped Lindsay and Mrs. Frost pick up the wrapping paper, ribbon, and cards from the floor. Lindsay proudly wore her new necklace. She gave Madison a hug.

"Thank you for everything," Lindsay whispered in Madison's ear. "Talking to you about the Big D and all that . . . well, it really helped me deal with today."

"Of course," Madison said. She gave Lindsay another big squeeze.

Aunt Mimi marched back into the living room with her hands in the air.

"Well, will wonders never cease?" she declared.

"What is it?" Mrs. Frost asked.

"That was George. Apparently, your father is downstairs, Lindsay."

Lindsay clutched her stomach. "He is? Really?"

"I told George to send him on up. He should be here in two shakes of a lamb's—"

Knock, knock, knock.

"That was fast," Aimee said.

All the color drained from Lindsay's cheeks. Mrs. Frost grabbed her daughter's hands.

"Look, Lindsay, I know you're angry with your father, and I understand your feelings. He has not been sensitive to your birthday and all your plans. You have every right to be mad."

"Mad?" Lindsay looked into her mom's eyes. "I'm not mad, Mom. I'm psyched. I wanted to see Dad. And he's here. He's here!"

As soon as Lindsay said that, she bounded toward the door.

Madison noticed how Mrs. Frost just stood there as if she'd been socked in the jaw.

Madison sat there, looking at the hurt expression on Mrs. Frost's face. Had Madison ever done that to her own mom—left her standing, abandoning her for a few moments with Dad?

Of course she had.

Madison knew from the guidance counselor at school that she couldn't control her parents' feelings.

134

She knew that the Big D wasn't *her* fault. But no matter how many times she heard that, she couldn't help thinking that a teeny-tiny part of her *was* to blame. And she knew that Lindsay felt the same way.

"Daddy!"

Everyone waited with anticipation for Mr. Frost to waltz into the living room where they were gathered. A moment later, he stumbled in—one arm wrapped around Lindsay's shoulder. Madison thought it looked as though Lindsay were about to cry again. But these were happy tears.

"Everyone, this is Dad, well, *my* dad," Lindsay said, introducing him to everyone in the room.

Mrs. Frost stood off to the side. Aunt Mimi stood next to her, with arms crossed. Madison knew those poses. She'd seen them many times before on her own mom when her dad came to pick her up. Even when Mom said hello in a nice voice, her body would show her discomfort.

"I don't get it," Aimee whispered to Fiona. "If your dad ditched you on your birthday, would you be acting all lovey-dovey?"

"No way. I don't get it, either," Fiona replied in an even softer whisper.

Madison overheard them but was too far from them to whisper herself. She stared down at her feet.

They didn't get it? Madison got it. She knew only

too well what it felt like to be rip-roaring mad at her father—and to love him way too much at the same time. In many ways, Lindsay and Madison were a lot more alike, a lot more like sisters, than either had imagined.

"Let me first say what a pleasure it is to finally meet all of your friends," Mr. Frost gasped, finally addressing everyone. His suit was a little rumpled, and he carried a briefcase that had a lock on one side. "Hello, Mimi. Hello, Jahnna."

Mr. Frost removed his suit jacket and placed it gingerly on a chair.

"Of course, I owe all of you an apology. Especially you, Lindsay. I have clients in from Tokyo, and an early meeting today turned into a marathon affair with an after-work dinner that I needed to show my face at—"

"I think we get the picture, Allan," Mrs. Frost said in a voice that was . . . well . . . *frosty*.

Before Mr. Frost could reply, Lindsay spoke up.

"Oh, Daddy, I knew you would come. We all did."

"Yes! Well!" Aunt Mimi clapped her hands. "Why don't you take a seat with the rest of us, Allan, and stay a spell?"

"I know it's late," Mr. Frost said, apologizing again as he took a seat. "I am so sorry that I missed the dinner party. Did you have a good time? Did you get any presents?" he asked Lindsay.

Lindsay nodded and turned toward her friends.

"Dad, this was the best birthday ever. They even told me so. And I got a book and . . ."

Lindsay's voice trailed off just a little bit as she grabbed her gifts and started to show them to her father.

"Wait! Before you do that," Mr. Frost interrupted, "I have something for you, too." He leaned over and produced a large yellow envelope from his jacket pocket. It was sealed with a gold foil sticker.

Everyone stared intently as Lindsay opened it.

"Wow!" Lindsay cried. She pulled out two tickets. "Theater tickets," she said. "It's just what I wanted."

"Uh-oh," Aimee said out loud without realizing it.

Fiona and Madison both gave her a nudge at the same time.

Dad grinned. "We can go to a show together," he said, "and maybe grab some dinner."

Madison watched as Mr. Frost told Lindsay about all the things they could do together, knowing that half of what he was talking about would probably never happen. At least that was how it had worked when Madison's parents had gotten divorced.

From across the room, Mrs. Frost watched her soon-to-be-ex-husband talking. Madison spotted her fidgeting, clearly uncomfortable being in the same room with him for very long. And even though Madison's experiences with the Big D had happened a year ago, she never stopped wondering why marriages had to come to this place, where two people who had once professed love now acted so cold, or in this case, frosty, with each other.

Lindsay and her father decided to throw on their jackets and head out to the terrace of Aunt Mimi's apartment. Madison, Aimee, and Fiona watched as their friend and her father huddled together against the cold outside, talking. Mrs. Frost went into the den to watch some TV. Aunt Mimi picked up in the living room and sent everyone else into the library, where she had an entertainment center, complete with DVDs and music.

Right away, Aimee found a recording of Tchaikovsky's *Nutcracker* Suite, one of her favorite ballets. She'd played a nutcracker and a mouse in performances of it; and more than anything, Aimee wanted to play the role of the little girl, maybe even in New York City. She knew that that was a big, big dream.

Madison spied the telephone sitting on a table in the corner of the room. She remembered that Aunt Mimi had said the kids could use the phones whenever they wanted, provided that they weren't calling anywhere crazy and talking long-distance for hours.

"Hey, Aim? Fiona? Can you turn the music down? I'm going to make a call," Madison said as she picked up the receiver. She dialed Far Hills. The phone rang.

"Are you calling home?" Aimee asked.

"She's probably calling Phinnie," Fiona said.

Someone picked up on the other end.

"Hello?" a voice said.

"Hello . . . Dad?" Madison said into the phone.

After everything that had happened to Lindsay, Madison needed to talk to her own father, too. After all, this would have been their usual night together. She needed to tell him how much she missed him and loved him. And of course, while she was at it, she'd tell him all about the Frrrozen hot chocolate, the makeovers, and the planetarium, too.

When Madison was finished talking, Aimee and Fiona decided it would be a good idea for them to call their fathers, too. By the time everyone had finished gabbing, Lindsay reappeared.

"My dad is leaving now," she said, sounding very sad.

"It's so great that he showed," Aimee said.

"I know," Lindsay said. "My mom is still mad at him, though."

"That's okay," Madison said. "That's how moms get."

"Lindsay, thank you for letting us be here," Fiona said.

"You keep saying that!" Lindsay said. She turned toward the DVD player. "Want to watch a movie?"

Aimee nodded emphatically. "Yeah, let's watch something scary."

"What?" Madison cried. "Aim, you get scared if someone goes, 'Boo'! Let's watch something mushy."

"A romantic movie will make me think of Egg," Fiona said sweetly.

Everyone pretended to gag.

"Cut it out!" Fiona cried. "I can't help it if I like him. Aim, you like Ben. Maddie, you like Hart."

"You know, I like someone, too," Lindsay admitted. Her three BFFs shot her a look.

"Who?" they asked.

Lindsay pressed her palms together and took a deep breath. "You promise you won't tell?"

Aimee laughed. "Tell who? We're it."

"Okay," Lindsay said. "I hardly ever think about guys this way. But . . ."

"Start talking!" Fiona said.

"I have this crush on . . . well . . . just a little crush, really . . . on . . ." she looked flustered as she tried to get the name out. "Dan. Ginsburg. I mean, he's always funny and nice, and he talks about books with me sometimes in the library."

There was total silence in the room.

Then Madison grinned. "Dan?"

Madison remembered a time when Dan had admitted that he liked *her*—during a school dance. But she'd wanted to stay just friends. It had been at that exact moment that Madison had admitted to herself just how much she liked Hart Jones.

"I can't believe you never told me that, Lindsay," Madison added.

"Well, no one ever really asked me whom I like. . . ." Lindsay said.

"I'm sorry!" Fiona blurted. "We're supposed to do that. I feel so silly. We're your friends, and we didn't ask. . . ."

"I'm sorry, too," Aimee said. "And I was going on about Ben yesterday."

"You never told me any of this?" Madison said to Lindsay. "Not even after all of our long talks. Whoa. I'm really surprised."

"It's really not a big deal, Maddie," Lindsay said. "But, since everyone seems to have someone to like, well, I just don't want to be left out, especially not on my birthday."

There was more to that statement, Madison knew, than just the fact that Lindsay liked Dan. She knew Lindsay didn't want to be left out by her dad or her mom, either, especially not during the Big D. Madison went over to Lindsay, grabbed her by the shoulders, and looked her square in the eye.

"Lindsay, you are not left out. Not ever. You are always super nice, and you're the queen of gossip, and your Aunt Mimi is the coolest aunt *ever*, and your dad showed up to celebrate your birthday. Your life is golden."

"Well . . ." Lindsay stammered. "My mom says all that glitters is not gold."

"Says who?" Aimee cried.

"Yeah!" Madison threw her arms into the air in a

141

funny imitation of Aunt Mimi. "All that glitters *is* gold, gold, gold. Abso-tootly!" she cried.

Everyone collapsed, laughing, onto the floor in front of the TV set.

"Let's watch the movie," Aimee said, holding up a DVD and then sliding it into the machine.

"A little romance it is," Lindsay said as she pushed PLAY.

142

Chapter 12

From: Bigwheels
To: MadFinn
Subject: How's the Party???
Date: Sat 12 Dec 11:01 PM

Hey there. Sorry I didn't write
again sooner than now. It has been
an insane wk @ school and home like
I said in my blog & my last E-M. I
am so jealous that ur in NYC right
now w/yr BFFs having the best TOYL!
I'm stuck here in the cold and it
really stinks. Ugh.

BUT did I tell u that the guy I
like, Reggie, gave me a stuffed

bear? He did last wk. I forgot to
say that. It's purple with this
ribbon on its neck that sparkles
and a silver satin flower on its
belly. I LOVE IT. Is it possible to
be in real love even though we're
in seventh grade? I wonder stuff
like that all the time. I know u
do 2. Like from everything you say
it sounds like Hart is THE one. But
how can we say that when we're
only 12? Is that a scary thought or
cool 4 u? My friend Lainie would
freak at the thought. She doesn't
even really LIKE boys. She never
has gone out with one or followed
one in school or even said much
about thinking they're cute. She'd
rather go to the stables with her
horse. Of course that's cool too.
We hung out yesterday and I helped
her groom her horse Tuck. Have u
ever ridden a horse? We don't go
that much b/c my mom is allergic.

N E WAY!

U have 2 write me ALL the details
about yr city trip. Can u send me a
New York E-card? Did u take digital
photos? I know yr mom and dad are

not too cool w/sending those online so LMK. My teacher at school always sez BSTS!

Write back sooooooooon!

Yours till the birth days,

Vicki aka Bigwheels

Madison clicked REPLY and sent Bigwheels a quick note back. Bigwheels had been right about the photographs. Mom had told Madison that she didn't want personal photos published online unless Madison could confirm the fact that the site was protected, and Madison couldn't very well do that from here. Maybe her dad could help her print out some of the photos that Aunt Mimi had taken at Serendipity and everywhere else—and Madison could make a collage later?

She looked over at the bed where Lindsay was snoring, fast asleep, with her feet poking out from under the blanket.

She tapped another few keys and opened a file.

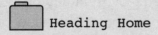 Heading Home

I want to come to New York for MY birthday party. Of course it would be great to rent Aunt Mimi for it, too, but I don't know if she's available. LOL.

Mom called this morning. She wanted to know when our train was getting back to Far Hills today. Aimee's mom is coming to pick up me and her. Fiona's dad is picking her up at the station with Chet b/c they have to go to church or something. I asked Lindsay if she wanted to sleep over @ my house tonight and she can't. But she's coming next weekend. I want to be here for her as much as possible so she doesn't get all sad and stressed out too much. I realize that I had Aimee and Lindsay around when MY parents went through the Big D, but no one was going through exactly what I was. That would have made a diff.

"Oh, no!"

Madison jumped. Lindsay had awakened with a shout. She turned to the side of the bed and scrambled onto the floor.

"Oh, no, Maddie! Oh, no! *Oh, no!*"

"What's the matter?" Madison was worried. She had expected Lindsay to wake up happy that morning. But instead, she seemed more freaked out than before.

"The test!" Lindsay cried. "With all my birthday-party stuff and worrying about my dad and watching movies, I forgot all about the standardized test at school!"

Madison clicked her laptop shut. Lindsay was right; Madison had forgotten about the test, too.

146

"We still have time to study," Madison said, "don't we?"

Aimee and Fiona stumbled into the bedroom, rubbing their eyes.

"Who screamed?" Aimee said. "I can't believe I slept this late."

Fiona yawned. "What happened?"

"The test," Lindsay said quickly. "We forgot to study." By now she was fishing in her bag for the books she'd brought along to study. "These books were right here the whole weekend. How could I have forgotten to even take them out and look at them once? Oh, no, what are we going to do?"

"Calm down, Lindsay," Aimee said, rushing over to her friend. "We can study today. And it doesn't matter, anyway. It's only a practice test."

"How are we supposed to study today?" Lindsay said, still sounding panicked. "We have to get ready and take the train back to Far Hills and . . ." She dissolved into tears.

"What's going on in here?" Aunt Mimi appeared at the doorway to the bedroom. In her hand was a large cake with lit candles.

"Look at that!" Fiona screeched.

Lindsay sniffled and looked at the cake. She wiped her eyes as everyone began to sing.

"Happy Birthday to you, Happy Birthday to you . . ."

"Make a wish, sweetheart," Mrs. Frost said,

stepping into the room and taking Lindsay's hands in hers.

"You already did this last night," Lindsay said.

"But you never made a wish," Fiona said.

Lindsay leaned over the cake, blinked, and blew out the candles.

"Happy Birthday to our BFF!" Aimee shouted, clapping loudly.

"What was your wish?" Fiona asked.

"She can't tell!" Madison cried. Ultrasuperstitious, Madison was certain that if a person revealed a wish out loud, then it would not happen. "Lindsay, you have to keep your wish a secret until some time passes and it has an opportunity to come true."

Lindsay, who had stopped crying completely by then, took a deep breath. "Maddie," she said. "It's not like my wish is really any big secret. I just wished that we all got a good grade on the standardized test."

"You wasted a perfectly good wish on *that*?" Aimee said.

Fiona laughed. "I thought you'd wish that Dan would like you back."

Lindsay's eyes bugged out.

"Dan?" Mrs. Frost asked. "Who's Dan?"

Lindsay froze. She didn't know what to say. No one did.

"Lindsay, is there some boy you're not telling me about?" Mrs. Frost asked sternly.

"Aw, it's probably just some movie star," Aunt Mimi said quickly, winking at Lindsay and her friends. "You know how it is with these gals. . . ."

"Oh?" Mrs. Frost said.

Madison reached over to squeeze Lindsay's hand. "Dan is this guy on TV. . . ." Madison started to say.

"Yeah, Mom," Lindsay said. "He's on this cable show I like. Remember?"

"He is? You told me?" Mrs. Frost asked, a bit flustered. "I see."

"Well, time to cut the cake," Aunt Mimi said, carting it back toward the door. "Meet me in the kitchen, everyone, so we can have cake for breakfast—just like I promised."

Mrs. Frost grabbed her daughter and gave her a warm embrace. "I love you, Lindsay," she said. "I'm sorry about last night. If I seemed angry, I apologize. I was just mad at your father for . . ."

"Mom, it's okay," Lindsay said. "Dad said he was sorry, too. I know things are weird right now. I understand."

Madison was happy to hear Lindsay say that. She was also happy to know that in exactly five minutes she would be taking a big, moist bite of white cake with purple icing. Birthday cake was a great way to start the new day.

Of course, Madison had to chuckle when she saw Lindsay grab the test-review book before heading toward the kitchen. Her friend was determined to study that morning—birthday celebration or not.

At Grand Central Station, everyone lugged their bags down the ramp toward the train. Aunt Mimi and Mrs. Frost had come along to help—and to say their good-byes. Mrs. Frost was going to drive back, but Lindsay wanted to take the train with her friends. She was going to hang out with Madison for a little while until her mom got back to Far Hills.

"Thank you so much for a fab weekend," Fiona said as she stepped aboard the train, blowing Aunt Mimi and Mrs. Frost a giant kiss.

"From me, too," Aimee said, leaning in for her own kiss.

"Don't forget to let me know if you want to bring your mom, and we can get a group together for the ballet," Aunt Mimi said.

Aimee smiled. "Sure thing," she said.

Madison hobbled over with her bags to say good-bye.

"Thanks, Mrs. Frost," she said, her voice practically a whisper. "And Aunt Mimi, thank you, too. I've never enjoyed New York City so much as I did this weekend."

"I know how much Lindsay values your friendship," Mrs. Frost said. "She always has."

Madison nodded. "Me, too. I like being sort-of sisters."

"Sisters are de-lish," Aunt Mimi said, taking Mrs. Frost by the arm. "Just look at us. Girlfriends till the end!"

Mrs. Frost laughed. "When I can keep up with her, that is."

"Bye!" Madison called out.

Madison, Aimee, and Fiona found seats very close to the door. They watched through the window as Lindsay said a more private good-bye to her mother and Aunt Mimi. Outside the train, more and more people began to gather. It was getting closer to departure time.

The air inside the train car had a coffee aroma. Madison loved that smell. It made her think of rainy Sundays at Dad's apartment, waking up late to eat Dad's famous breakfast of scrambled eggs and raisin toast and then go for a long, wet walk with Phinnie. She was glad that Dad had agreed to pick her up at the train station when they got back to Far Hills. Madison had told him on the telephone that she wanted to sleep over at his house that night.

The train lights flashed. A loud ping meant the doors were about to shut.

"Lindsay! Lindsay!" Madison, Aimee, and Fiona banged on the window at the same time. She couldn't hear them, but she was coming. Of course, Lindsay had heard the ping, too.

The friends watched as Lindsay kissed and hugged her mom and aunt once each. Then she hugged them again. She grabbed her one small bag (Mrs. Frost had taken the rest, including the birthday gifts, to bring by car). Then she hopped on, in the nick of time.

As the train pulled out of the station, Madison gazed out at Lindsay's mother and at Aunt Mimi, whose arms were linked as they waved back at the girls. Although the station was murky and dirty, the two sisters seemed to sparkle, standing there on the platform. Maybe it was the buttons on their coats. Maybe it was their hair clips. Madison wasn't sure what it was. But in that moment, Aunt Mimi and Mrs. Frost glittered as brightly as anything in all of New York City.

"So," Lindsay said as soon as they'd settled into their seats and given the conductor their tickets. "Let's study."

Aimee was sleepy. "I'm too tired to work," she said. "Let's just space out or play MASH or Truth or Dare."

"I think maybe we should study a little bit," Fiona said. "Just in case."

"I think so, too," Madison said.

"Fine," Aimee said. "So what are we supposed to do?"

Lindsay opened a book called *All You Need to Know About Standardized Tests*. It was stamped SEVENTH-GRADE EDITION.

152

"This is the best book for us to use," Lindsay said.

"You're way too organized," Aimee said. "That's at least a hundred pages long."

"It's three hundred pages. But I've only read it through a few times," Lindsay said.

"Are you kidding me?" Aimee asked. "You've already read it a few times? What are you freaking out about, then?"

Fiona giggled. So did Madison.

"Lindsay, you really are such a worrywart," Madison said. "It's just a practice test."

"I know, I know!" Lindsay said. "But at least I'm a *prepared* worrywart."

They quizzed each other on a variety of subjects: rational and real numbers; geometry; cell biology; geology; the Renaissance; U.S. history; sentence structure; and even the vocabulary of technology. Madison was especially good at the last part. She hadn't realized that learning HTML would actually help her on a school test one day.

"I hope there isn't too much reading comprehension," Fiona grumbled. "I always make mistakes on those questions. I don't know why."

"I hope they don't ask a lot of questions about history," Madison said. "I get confused between the Age of Reason and the Age of Enlightenment."

"Oh, I hope they do ask a lot of history questions," Lindsay said. "I'm way better at that than I am at remembering math."

"Wait! What's the Pythagorean theorem again?" Aimee asked.

Fiona knew that answer. "For a right triangle with legs a and b and hypotenuse c, the formula is a-squared plus b-squared equals c-squared. Right?"

Lindsay made a face. "Yeah, you're right. Ugh. I hope I pass this . . ."

"I think we'll *all* do great," Madison said to cheer everyone up. "We'll do better than Poison Ivy. She never studies for real for anything . . ."

"And don't forget Lance," Aimee said.

"Or my brother Chet," Fiona said with a giggle. "Even if he studies, he probably will mess up."

"Well, at least we tried," Madison said. It was the kind of thing her Gramma Helen would have said.

All the practicing and quizzing made the time pass very quickly. The train pulled into the station at Far Hills around two o'clock.

As they exited the train, Madison saw the parents clustered together: Mrs. Gillespie, Mr. Waters, and Madison's dad, too. Dad had brought Phinnie along, and the dog started tugging at his leash the moment he saw Madison appear.

The girls said their various good-byes and headed for home. Aimee and Fiona promised to e-mail Madison later. They were curious to know if Hart had sent any notes or left any messages at Madison's house.

"I'm so glad you called me yesterday," Dad told Madison in the car as he pulled away.

"Me, too," Madison said.

She and Lindsay huddled together in the back-seat with Phinnie, who couldn't stop licking Madison's hands and face. His little pug tail was wagging nonstop.

"It sounds like you had yourselves quite a terrific weekend," Dad said, looking at them in the rearview mirror.

"It was the best," Lindsay said, squeezing Madison's hand. "But it's always the best when your best friends are there."

Chapter 13

 Wonder

It is now so early in the morning that the sun hasn't even totally come out yet. I can see it through the window here @ Dad's place. It's coming in like slivers of light through the blinds. I keep thinking about the sun and all the planets out there somewhere, so far away, like our moon and the moons of Jupiter. It makes me wonder.

Rude Awakening: This weekend we saw a thousand lights glittering in the planetarium. But somehow, I still feel like I'm in the dark.

There is SO much I don't know--about all those stars up in the sky, about the test coming up, and even about whether or not Hart Jones really likes me enough to ask me out again.

"Maddie?" a voice croaked from the dark hallway outside Madison's room. It was Madison's stepmother, Stephanie. She'd just gotten up to prepare for work. She had an appointment in another county—and a long drive ahead of her that morning. Her hair was pulled up in a barrette and she was wearing only a long T-shirt and her slippers.

"Hey, Stephanie," Madison said in a low voice. Phinnie was still asleep, on top of Madison's bed.

"What are you doing up this early?" Stephanie asked. "You're always on the computer, aren't you?"

"Not always," Madison said. "Is Dad up?"

"Not yet. He's out cold," Stephanie said. "The alarm will be going off in about a half hour."

"I couldn't sleep anymore. And then I saw the sunrise," Madison explained, pointing to the window.

Stephanie walked into Madison's room and pulled open one of the blinds. Beautiful morning light poured into the room, and everything was bathed in Madison's favorite color, orange.

"Mmmm," Stephanie cooed. "That's a nice way to greet the day."

Madison grinned. "I'm glad I slept over," she said.

"So are we," Stephanie said. "Your dad, especially.

157

He really misses you when plans change and he can't do the regular dinners. It was all he talked about on Saturday night."

"Really?" Madison said.

"Well, I'd better get into the shower," Stephanie said. She kissed Madison on the top of the head. "There's fresh OJ in the fridge if you want to pour yourself a glass."

"Thanks," Madison said, turning back to her laptop. She realized, after she saved the file in which she had been writing, that she hadn't checked her e-mailbox since the other night at Aunt Mimi's apartment. Madison quickly surfed into bigfishbowl.com and opened it up.

FROM	SUBJECT
✉ XMENALOT	Special Offer
✉ GoGramma	Miss You
✉ Bigwheels	RE: What If
✉ Wetwinz	Egg Says . . .
✉ LuvNstuff	Thank you!!!
✉ Sk8ingboy	Try This FREE

She couldn't believe that she'd received so much mail in only a day. The first one was an easy delete. It was clearly spam. The message from Gramma Helen was short and sweet. Madison would write her back later, maybe in the media lab at school, after the dreaded test. Then Madison opened the note from Bigwheels.

From: Bigwheels
To: MadFinn
Subject: RE: What If
Date: Sun 13 Dec 8:10 PM

My brother said a few words today.
Not just one--but three--MAMA,
DADDO, and ME-ME. We were all
amazed. Madison, you don't know how
cool this is for my mom & dad. Mom
says I can keep my blog going, BTW,
so check back for more news--and
more words YEAH!

On top of everything else, I found
out that we don't have to take any
more tests @ school this week. I'm
sorry you do. You will ACE THEM
ALL! I know it. :-l

Write back SOON.

Yours till the hot chocolates (your
frozen kind sounds so yummy!)

Vicki aka Bigwheels

Madison hit SAVE so she would remember to write
Bigwheels later that day. She clicked on Fiona's
e-mail next, hoping for some good news about the
whole Hart situation.

From: Wetwinz
To: MadFinn, BalletGrl, LuvNstuff
Subject: Egg Says . . .
Date: Mon 1 Dec 12:08 AM
_____
I can't believe I'm online right
now OMG! But earlier tonite Egg
called me & I had 2 share w/u. He
says that the test is supposed to
be super EZ. His sister Mariah took
it 2 yrs ago and she didn't have
any probs. Aim--what about yr bros?
Did u ask them? We should have
thought of that on Friday! Ok so
CUL8R.

xoxo

F.

Madison hit DELETE. She had hoped for a different
kind of news, but apparently, Hart had not told Egg
anything. Or at least, Fiona wasn't saying.

The next e-mail was from Lindsay. Madison opened
it up: the attachment was an E-card from one of those
cool free greeting-card sites. It played music and had
an animation of a frog leaping across lily pads. A
shower of virtual confetti sprinkled across the screen
once the card was read. Madison couldn't believe that
Lindsay had sent a thank-you card already.

The last e-mail in Madison's e-mailbox looked like

spam, too. She didn't recognize the address or the subject matter. But then she looked a little bit closer at the sender's name.

✉ HartUR4E   Try This FREE

She couldn't believe the coincidence. How had Hart's name—of all names—ended up in her e-mailbox? She thought back to something Aunt Mimi had said that weekend, about not believing in coincidences. Aunt Mimi believed in destiny. Madison wanted to believe in destiny, too—as in, her destiny with Hart. So she didn't open the message, just in case there was a virus contained in it, but she also didn't delete it, just in case it meant something.

Morale at school that morning was low. Signs were posted all over FHJH telling students about the times and locations of their particular standardized-test practices. Most of them took place in people's first-period classes. Madison couldn't believe that. Her first period today was Science. That meant she had to take the test with her enemy, Poison Ivy.

Before heading off to class, Madison, Aimee, Fiona, and Lindsay met up by the lockers for a good-luck hug. They agreed that everyone would get together later in the cafeteria to exchange thoughts about what had happened during the test. Aimee made Lindsay promise them all that she would not freak out in the middle of the test if she didn't know an answer.

Mr. Danehy stood at the front of Madison's science classroom with a sour look on his face, waiting for the bell to ring.

Madison slid into her seat. Ivy wasn't there! She couldn't believe her luck. No enemy, no problem. Another reason she was glad that Ivy was missing was that she wouldn't have to deal with any more obscure accusations concerning missing (or stolen) notebooks. That morning Madison had *not* found Ivy's notebook in her locker.

"Please put your bags under your chairs." Mr. Danehy started his speech about test rules. The class had heard a version of these rules at least a hundred times before.

Madison stared across the room while Mr. Danehy was speaking. Her eyes landed on something familiar. Well, some*one* familiar.

Hart was looking back at her. He smiled.

Madison smiled, too. Her entire body warmed up when she did that. It was a strange sensation. Normally, Hart made her nervous, but for some reason, looking at him right now, before the big practice test, she relaxed.

Everyone got settled in their seats with sharpened pencils. A few moments after the class bell rang, Mr. Danehy formally began the test with a smack of his palm on his desk. "Go!" he cried.

Most of the kids laughed nervously. Madison just stared straight down at the page. She wanted to get this over with as fast as possible.

There weren't too many questions on computer technology, which was a bummer, but there were questions on the Age of Enlightenment and the Age of Reason. Thanks to a study trick that Lindsay had shared on the train, Madison got both questions right. Or at least, she was pretty sure she did. She zipped through most of the math section, too. Egg's sister, Mariah, had given good advice. This was a lot easier than it seemed.

At lunchtime, Madison couldn't wait to catch up with Aimee, Fiona, Lindsay, and the others to exchange reactions. Since it was just a practice test, the results didn't *really* matter, except that it meant something among friends. Even if the grades didn't count on people's report cards, they counted when being compared with those of other kids in the class.

Madison didn't usually feel so competitive about that kind of thing, but even she found herself wanting an excellent score so she would have bragging rights. She hoped that Lindsay, however, got the best score of all. Lindsay needed bragging rights more than anyone. Of all her friends, Lindsay was the one who counted on the A-pluses. Of course, minus signs next to grade letters were unacceptable. And after a stressful (although very fun!) birthday weekend, Madison knew that a perfect (or nearly perfect) test score would be a most excellent bonus birthday present.

The friends met up with lunch trays and headed for the orange table at the back of the cafeteria. The girls sat together, but as it worked out, Hart Jones ended up sitting directly across from Madison.

"How did you do?" Madison asked him.

Hart shrugged. He'd smiled before in the class-room, but now he was grunting, not even saying real words, and playing with the food on his lunch tray.

Madison stared as he ate three bites of his turkey sandwich. Still, Hart said nothing.

Aimee leaned over to Madison. "Gee, he's real talkative today," she murmured.

Madison nodded. "I know," she said.

Fiona and Chet started bickering about one of the test questions. Chet thought he had chosen the right answer, but his sister told him that he was wrong. Fiona loved telling Chet he was wrong.

"Hart," Drew said. "You want to check with Coach about hockey this weekend?" He stood up holding his backpack. Hart stood up, too.

"See you later, gator," Egg said. He touched Fiona's shoulder and gave Drew a high five. Madison noticed that, and it gave her a little twinge in the pit of her stomach. Egg and Fiona were sitting there like a couple while Madison's crush was walking away.

"So long," Hart said to everyone at the table. "You too, Finnster," he said softly.

Madison sat up a little bit straighter. "Oh . . .

bye," she said, still wondering why Hart was acting so strange.

Now the only kids left at the orange table were Chet, Egg, and the four girlfriends.

Aimee picked at the rest of her lunch. Lindsay swiped a carrot stick from Fiona's tray and took a bite.

From out of nowhere, Dan Ginsburg appeared. "Where are the other guys?" he asked as he pulled up the bench and slid his lunch tray onto the table.

Madison, Aimee, and Fiona quickly turned at the exact same time and stared right at Lindsay.

Lindsay looked down at her tray. She didn't know what to say. All the attention had somehow shifted her way, and she became self-conscious.

So did Dan.

"Um . . . what's up, Egg?" Dan asked.

Egg grunted. "Not much, man. Lunch today is gross. Don't eat that lasagna. It was moving. I swear."

Madison looked over at Lindsay again.

Dan shifted in his own seat. "What's going on?" he asked, confused by all the furtive glances and the silences. "Who died?"

Chet threw a piece of corn at Dan's head. Dan laughed, sounding relieved, and then tossed back a roll. Then Egg joined in with a grape. Soon all three boys broke into a mini–food fight. Luckily there were no lunch monitors in the area.

"I think I'd better go," Madison said, standing up amid the mess.

"I'll come with you," Lindsay said.

Fiona decided to stay with Egg and the others. Aimee was staying, too.

"See you after classes," they said to Madison and Lindsay.

"I was ready to throw food at *you*!" Lindsay whispered as she walked away from the table with Madison. "Am I blushing? I have never been so embarrassed—never!"

"I couldn't help it," Madison said with a giggle. "I'm sorry, Lindsay, but you told us that stuff about Dan the other day, and then he walked up to the table, and . . . well, we all lost our cool. Sorry. Really. Sorry."

"Oh, I don't really care," Lindsay said. "It just felt weird, that's all. Do you think he knows how I feel?"

Madison shook her head. "No way," she said quickly, unsure if that was the right response. "But I bet once he knows, he'll be happy about it," she added.

Lindsay seemed pleased with that answer.

As they walked out of the cafeteria, Madison noticed that neither Ivy nor the drones seemed to be at school. They weren't sitting at their usual lunch table and they hadn't been in morning classes, either. Madison figured they had probably decided to play hooky to avoid the test. She wondered who was smarter: Lindsay, for studying for the practice test—or Ivy, Rose, and Joan, for not even showing up.

Madison and Lindsay made their way down the corridor toward the lockers. Madison opened hers and pulled out a math textbook for an afternoon class.

Lindsay stood at her locker a few feet away. "Oh, my gosh!" she cried out. "I can't believe I forgot to show you this at lunch."

Madison had to smile. Lindsay showed her a printout of one of Aunt Mimi's digital photos from the party weekend. It was the shot of all four friends standing under the sign that read MADISON AVENUE.

"It's for you," Lindsay said. "I have copies for everyone."

Madison gave Lindsay a hug. "I'm sticking it up on my locker right now," she said. She reached into her orange bag. "Wait, I know I have tape somewhere inside here. Maybe at the bottom . . . somewhere . . ."

She reached around inside the bottom of the bag but didn't find the tape right away.

"Paper clip . . . quarter . . . pencil—ouch! I just sharpened it . . . let's see . . . here's the tape. It's stuck under one of my books. . . ."

With one pull, Madison produced the tape. Along with it, however, some other things slipped out.

"What a mess. I need to clean my bag," Madison said. "I have so much stuff."

One of the items that flew out was the copy of Lindsay's birthday invitation. The pink-glitter envelope shimmered under the neon lights in the hallway. A few kids ran by on their way to their own lockers.

"What's this?" Lindsay asked. She handed Madison another envelope. This one was blue.

"I don't know," Madison said. "I didn't see that before."

On the front of the envelope was one word. Madison's stomach flip-flopped when she saw it.

Finnster.

"Open it! Open it!" Lindsay cried.

Madison wanted to tear it open, but her fingers didn't seem to work.

"You open it," she told Lindsay.

"Me? But . . ." Lindsay paused. "Maddie, this could be it."

"What?"

"It. You know."

"Open it, please," Madison begged.

Lindsay gently ripped one corner of the envelope. Out slid a note. It was a short one, Madison could tell.

"Give it to me!" Madison shouted, grabbing the note from Lindsay.

Lindsay burst into laughter. "Okay, okay. Here."

Madison felt her knees go weak. She slid down the locker bank to the floor, landing with a dull thud. Lindsay sat down next to her.

"Breathe, Maddie, breathe."

Madison peeled open the note.

Hey, I don't have hockey in a few weekends from now. My dad says he can take us to the movies. You wanna go then?

Hart

P.S.: Sorry about last week.

Madison's skin felt hot. Her eyes watered.

Lindsay looked into her BFF's face. "Maddie? Are you okay? What does the note say?"

"Everything," Madison said. She leaned into Lindsay and stared back at the note. "Everything."

Even though Hart had written on paper that was plain compared to Lindsay's pink-glitter invitation, it didn't matter.

Nothing mattered except for one thing.

Hart Jones had asked.

Madison was ready to say yes.

And Aimee was so right about what she had said after they went to the planetarium. They definitely were *not* alone in the galaxy—not anymore.

Mad Chat Words:

BLOGYL	Blog you later!
22C	Too, too cool
WHA?	What happened?
<:-Z	Uh-oh
IGI	I get it
FCF	Friends come first
Blahblahblah	Same old story
Dunno	I don't know
E-M	E-mail
TOYL	Time of your life
LMK	Let me know
BSTS	Better safe than sorry
Diff	Difference
:-1	So there!

Madison's Computer Tip

We got back from the weekend party at Lindsay's aunt Mimi's apartment and I was on a cloud. And then, just when I thought everything couldn't seem more perfect, I got this incredible thank-you note from Lindsay in my e-mail. **When you need to thank someone or send a birthday card or any greeting card, use an E-card service**. I think I am going to send E-cards now to everyone I know all the time. The music and animation make it so much cooler than a card you get in the mail. Although, as Gramma Helen would say, there's nothing like getting a real piece of mail. So I guess I'll send E-cards *and* regular cards. Wow, I'm going to be busy.

For a complete Mad Chat dictionary and more about Madison Finn, visit Madison at www.lauradower.com